JOÃO ALMINO

ENIGMAS OF SPRING

A Novel

Translated by Rhett McNeil

DALKEY ARCHIVE PRESS

Originally published in Portuguese as *Enigmas da Primavera* in 2015

© 2015 by João Almino
Translation copyright © 2016 by Rhett McNeil

First edition, 2016
All rights reserved

Library of Congress Cataloging-in-Publication Data

Names: Almino, João, author. | McNeil, Rhett, translator.
Title: Enigmas of spring / by João Almino ; translated by Rhett McNeil.
Other titles: Enigmas da primavera. English
Description: First edition. | Victoria, TX : Dalkey Archive Press, 2016.
Identifiers: LCCN 2015040715 | ISBN 9781628971316 (pbk. : alk. paper)
Classification: LCC PQ9698.1.L58 E513 2016 | DDC 869.3/42--dc23
LC record available at http://lccn.loc.gov/2015040715

ILLINOIS
ARTS
COUNCIL
AGENCY

Partially funded by the Illinois Arts Council, a state agency.

Dalkey Archive Press
Victoria, TX / McLean, IL / Dublin / London
www.dalkeyarchive.com

Dalkey Archive Press publications are, in part, made possible through the support of the University of Houston-Victoria
and its programs in creative writing, publishing, and translation.

Typesetting: Mikhail Iliatov
Cover: Art by Katherine O'Shea

Printed on permanent / durable acid-free paper.

I would like to thank my friends Antonio Maura, who read with astuteness and commented on the various levels of the text, and to whom I owe one of the epigraphs; Ángel Basanta, for his intelligent and precise analysis; Tadeu Valadares, Cristina Vieira, and, above all, my wife, Bia Wouk, who all helped me with revisions and a careful re-reading of the book; Ánuar Nahes and Luciana Villas-Boas, my agent, for attentive reading and suggestions; Sami Achcar, Paulo Daniel Farah, and Janan Habib, who answered my questions about the Arabic language and world; as well as my publisher in the English language, John O'Brien, for believing once more in my literature and for his support.

For Elisa and Letícia

Ainsi l'Islam qui, dans le Proche-Orient, fut
l'inventeur de la tolérance, pardonne mal aux
non-musulmans de ne pas abjurer leur foi au
profit de la sienne, puisqu'elle a sur toutes les
autres la supériorité écrasante de les respecter.
—Claude Lévi-Strauss, *Tristes tropiques*

Soy tuyo, por muy lejos que estés de mí.
Tu pena, cuando sufres, me da pesar a mí.
No hay soplo de viento que no me traiga
tu perfume.
No hay pájaro canoro que no pronuncie
tu nombre.
Cada recuerdo que ha dejado su huella en mí
permanece eternamente, como si fuera parte de mí.
—Nizâmî, *Layla y Majnún*
   (translated by Jordi Quingles)

La primavera ha venido.
Nadie sabe cómo ha sido.
—Antonio Machado, "Canciones"

Love returned to feed on the papers where,
absentmindedly, I again had written my name.
—João Cabral de Melo Neto, "The Three Unloved"

Chapter in which the hero of this story all but loses his head

In the arms of the fat woman in a black dress, her eyes lively and dark, he was nothing more than a head. No neck or torso or arms or legs. Just a head. With a beard and disheveled hair. He caught a glimpse of himself in the silver-framed mirror, dirty with sepia streaks: a head. He exhaled. The mirror fogged up.

The woman, with a scornful, satisfied smile, hugged his head and rested it between her breasts. Afterwards she put it on a table with metal legs and a glass top, delicately engraved with symbols and Arabic letters, which he tried in vain to decipher. The woman showed him a sheet of paper: "Make a drawing that contains the letter 'S' and the number seven." He had no arms, hands, or fingers. Even worse: he didn't have a pencil.

By force of imagination he sketched out a crude, ugly drawing, which the woman came over to look at. Ashamed, he nervously tried to erase it. He'd had something different in his head, a simpler design that contained, as she had requested, the letter and the number — distinct and clear, with no room for uncertainty.

Too late. He didn't have time to erase the imperfect drawing.

Now he was sitting near the edge of a well, whose depths reflected his anguished face. A child in front of him extended an arm and handed him *El libro de Dolores*, *The Book of Sorrows*.

Who was the young man sitting beside him, dressed in a brown-and-black plaid suit and a lipstick-red bowtie? He tried to ask: Who are you? But his voice didn't come out. He tried again. Nothing. His voice still wouldn't come out. And then it came out sounding like a hoarse rumble, like sounds produced with great effort by someone who has lost their voice from a stroke. The young man was no older than his own twenty years. Scowling, he took a seat in a warm, purple armchair, sweat running down his face. He lit a pipe. "I'm your destiny," the young man whispered in his ear, sitting down on the edge of the bed, which trembled from his weight.

Let's call our hero Majnun. Almost two and a half years had passed, and Majnun still remembered that dream. He had awoken frightened and naked. It wasn't a nightmare, the young man who had sat down beside him was too real, he wasn't a part of a dream. Naked in front of his computer, which lit up his beard, dark eyes, and oval-shaped head. Majnun was a nickname friends had given him. Or, more precisely, one female friend. And there was a reason behind it, which will become clear.

At the manifestation in front of the Congressional Building and Itamaraty Palace on June 20th 2013, he ran into Suzana. He hadn't seen her for a year and a half. He had traveled to Spain with her, but their families hadn't seen each other since the death of his grandfather Dario. Back then, another woman, Laila, had been his great passion.

Delirium of nascent love

He met Laila in early 2011, at a night out in the Setor de Oficinas neighborhood. From the moment their eyes met, they had no desire to look away. The freedom with which she looked at him was an invitation for him to get up and walk towards her, which he would have done immediately if he hadn't felt shy about talking to a woman whom he'd just seen for the first time.

What was this feeling that made him lose all sense of reason, morality, and reality? It wasn't admiration he felt for that stranger. Nor was it affection. It was something that, when experienced for the first time, was transmitted through the eyes like a fever, a sickness, perhaps a mortal one. His blood disappeared. He felt dizzy, like he might faint. It wasn't merely an attraction to that gaze or to the carnality revealed by the low neckline and the shiny dress that fit close against the shape of her body.

Accompanied by two girlfriends, she kept dancing intently out on the dance floor, a mystery in her venomous green gaze, desire emanating from her mouth. Her delicate lips traced a sly smile when he approached her. Then they started dancing, dancing. How to stop time? Majnun didn't know that she was dancing to take revenge on her husband. Nor that any husband even existed. He couldn't foresee all the turmoil that would follow.

When a slow song came on, she held him close. And they danced, fading into each other's embrace. Later on, outside the nightclub, in a dark corner, from which they heard the sounds of motorcycles in the distance and smelled the scent of grass and fertilizer, he was able to touch, underneath the long, green printed dress, the hairs between Laila's thick thighs. He liked the fat around her waist, which he imagined quivering during a belly dance in some distant place, perhaps Egypt or Lebanon. He wasn't named Qays, like the young man in the Eastern myth he'd read, but he had found his Laila. Might he have fallen in love with a name?

In the wee hours on the night Majnun first met Laila, when he arrived home, his grandma Elvira, a Pernambucan woman who had raised him in Brasilia, was waiting for him in the living room. She seemed to sense the beginnings of that wild passion. Whispered advice poured forth from her round, white face and pointed lips, as if she were telling him a secret:

"Live all that you can while there's still time to do it, my son. But remember that sex doesn't last a lifetime; affection is what matters in the long run."

His grandfather, Dario, was ten years older than her. They didn't agree on anything. They no longer had sex. These three factors explained what she had said, concluded Majnun on that distant night, back when he hadn't yet caused his grandfather the profound sorrow that had perhaps contributed to his death. But words that echoed stubbornly throbbed like pain. Elvira's words, were a curse upon his passion for Laila, married and fifteen years his senior.

"I don't want to be in love," Majnun thought. "But how can I combat these feelings that show up uninvited, with no advance notice?"

Since the death of his father, he had lived in a house in the Dom Bosco Manors neighborhood, an airy home with large open spaces and exposed beams and roof tiles, which had been built in the nineties. It combined Neocolonial and Mediterranean styles in the arches out on the back porch, which were supported by two columns. The wooden window frames, painted blue, contrasted with the white of the walls. The living room—luminous, with a vaulted ceiling, wooden beams, and floor-to-ceiling glass doors—was divided into two areas, beyond which was a dining room with a large, antique dinner table, purchased in Minas Gerais.

Majnun's bedroom gave out onto the back balcony, where, on a round iron table that overlooked the pool, he had developed the habit of taking his breakfast every morning, alongside his grandfather Dario.

He had been raised by Elvira and Dario, his maternal grandparents, ever since his father had died of an overdose, a father who had transmitted to him a tormented mind and a peculiar way of understanding the world. His father had gotten his mother pregnant when he was fifteen, his mother only sixteen. Addicted to heroin and given to psychotic breaks, she had long been institutionalized. For all intents and purposes, she didn't exist. On the few occasions that Majnun had seen her, she seemed troubled. Whenever he thought about her, he imagined her throwing back whiskeys and snorting lines of cocaine.

In the morning, his grandfather was always generously cologned and properly dressed in the discreet elegance of his suits and ties. Age had whitened his goatee and hair, but had had no effect on his slender figure or steadfast posture. Dario toked on his cigars with appetite and pleasure equal to that of a baby at its mother's breast. Smoke, cologne, and joy emanated from him, wafting throughout the room and onto the balcony.

Majnun's grandmother almost never joined them for breakfast, since she got started on the morning chores much earlier. The maid, who had also come from Pernambuco years before and treated him like a son, set the table. When Majnun stayed home, closed off in his bedroom, usually in front of the computer, she brought in juices and cakes, serving him with her calloused hands, without a word, so as not to interrupt his concentration. In June of 2013, before he left for the protests, she brought him two handkerchiefs and a small bottle of vinegar, good, she said, for counteracting the effects of tear gas.

A Carmen, but not Bizet's

The day after he first met Laila, in January of 2011, a Spanish professor — a friend of his grandfather — was set to arrive for a conference on medieval Spain. Dario had charged Majnun with stopping by the Hotel Nacional, where the University of Brasilia had put up the professor, to take him to campus. Some mysterious disposition had made Majnun feel an aversion to this professor even before meeting him, but it was soon transformed when he found out the subject of the conference and that the professor was also a specialist in Islamic studies. Perhaps because his paternal grandmother, Mona, the one who lived in São Paulo, had always been an inspiration to him, he had taken an early interest in Islamic culture and, among many of his impossible dreams, he dreamed of visiting — as if it still existed —medieval, Islamic Spain.

He was apprehensive, his mind divided. He saw himself arriving early at the hotel to exchange ideas with the professor and, at the same time, sitting in a seat in the back row of the auditorium, unable to formulate a single question. This hesitation filled him with desire, and this desire filled him with timidity.

Still feeling the impact of his encounter with Laila, he recalled every detail of her body hidden under that shiny dress. He kept coming back to her green, mysterious eyes, her smile, her reclined head, everything that spoke directly to his soul, if he even had a soul. The hours since he had left her side had dissolved into seconds, which brought Majnun anxiety more than pleasure; it was the melancholy of the enamored more than the joy of the adventurer. Laila was his uncertain and dangerous future. He didn't even understand himself, always caught up in visions of what he had experienced and, principally, what he might someday experience. But Laila understood him.

In the lobby of the hotel, a young woman with lively eyes looked over at him. She was black, skinny, and lanky; the opposite of Laila. She could have been one of those skeletons with an interesting face who sell lingerie and are worshipped by the fashion industry.

She went over to the reception desk, asked after Professor Rodrigo Díaz, and requested his room number so she could call him. The attractiveness of her features wasn't to be found in her dark eyes, her wide mouth, her fine chin, her flat nose, or her small ears; it was everything together, perhaps in the way that her eyes, mouth, chin, nose, and ears created, in perfect harmony, a sensation of tranquil happiness. She eventually asked Majnun:

"Are you also here to talk to Professor Rodrigo Díaz?"

"Yep. We're supposed to meet in the lobby. I've never met him," replied Majnun, adjusting on his shoulder the black canvas tote bag which contained his computer.

"I haven't either. I know his son, an architect who was here in Brasilia last year. The professor is on his way down."

They had merely exchanged a few words, but Majnun felt as if they were already old friends. He took note of her vague smile and the red lipstick on her thick lips.

"You don't recognize me, do you?" she said. "We met at Suzana's house."

Into his head popped—like images on a computer screen—a miniskirt, a tight dress, full breasts, brand-name shoes and purse: Suzana, a spoiled daddy's girl, whose father owned a rug shop. The image of Suzana, fixated on her body more than her spirit, shifted hesitatingly, as if he were trying to make some concession to reason, from her knees up to the smooth features of her face, bordered by blonde hair, which fell about her shoulders. A face on which vanity, applied with the best cosmetics, was prominently displayed, light and colorful. The image of happiness. It was possible to decipher her face without fear of misreading it, a face that revealed everything, open and sincere. Majnun could envisage, through her skimpy clothes, the look of her naked body, and he let his mind wander, embellishing her body with vices he believed it already possessed, adding on others that he thought would suit her well.

"Carmen, you're Carmen," he said, awaking from that vision with a modicum of pride at recalling their brief encounter at Suzana's party.

"Good memory. Why don't we have a seat?" she said, inviting him to sit in a black chair facing the elevators.

"I think I'll recognize the professor. I googled some pictures of him," said Majnun. "Are you going to the conference?"

"No. That's not my scene. I came to drop off something for Pablo, his son."

Carmen went over to the window that gave out onto the street and looked at something outside. Had he responded coldly to her friendliness, making her prefer to wait alone in the hotel lobby? Pretending to read on his laptop, he noticed Carmen examining him with a look of superiority, dissecting him from top to bottom. She knew him, knew him inside out, divined his weaknesses, his timidity, his fear, and his passivity; a passivity that disturbed him, and which he assumed was impossible to eradicate, since it was specific to his times. What he still didn't know was that an era can change its spots.

To fill the void with the appearance of action, he fixed his eyes back on his laptop screen. He adjusted himself in the chair, bothered by something he couldn't quite understand. Or he did understand it. Confronted with any woman that caught his interest, he thought about how she might see him: his thick, black, unkempt beard, his oval-shaped head, his skinny, short body, his mountain of disheveled hair, his prominent nose, his glasses, which were much too big for his pale face, his sloppy shorts, which went halfway down his shin.

Carmen dressed in the same casual manner, but on her this carelessness became elegance. Was she older than him? Certainly not as much older as Laila was.

"Here's my business card," she said, walking back over to him.

On it, he read: "Carmen Silva, Catering," an address in the neighboring city of Taguatinga, a phone number, and her email address.

Impossible Causes

"I would like to have lived in the Alhambra, in Granada," said Majnun to the professor in the car on their way to the University of Brasilia.

Rodrigo Díaz was straightening his thin hair and well-trimmed beard—both completely white—with his right hand, on which he wore a gold ring, perhaps a class ring. Majnun knew very little about him: that his wife, from whom he had been separated for years, had died of cancer three years earlier; that his daughter, a biologist, lived in Switzerland with her husband; and that he had an architect son named Pablo.

"You're not the first, but don't idealize Granada," counseled the professor in a serious, nasal voice.

"I once wrote," said Majnun, full of himself, "that 'my fear and my hope reside in Brasilia; my passion, in Granada.' I'm writing a short story—actually, it's now a novella—about the Alhambra and . . ."

"You write?"

"Well, I've never published anything."

"There's no rush. What are you studying?"

"I failed the history entrance exam."

Majnun lowered his head and raised a hand up to his eyes, embarrassed. He interpreted the silence that followed as censure or contempt. Then he raised his head, filled his lungs with air in order to suppress that feeling of defeat, and said, smiling:

"My novel is also about . . . I mean, I intend to include an essay on Islamic tolerance in the novella."

He had submitted an early, abbreviated version of the novella, in the form of a short story, to a contest.

"You might be able to get something out of this series of lectures. We're going to talk about tolerance, but I know that at least one of the presentations will touch on the subject of the massacres of Jews."

"I know that . . ."

Professor Rodrigo didn't hear him and continued:

"It was also commonplace during that era for enemy prisoners to be taken as slaves. Innumerable stories of Christian prisoners in Granada."

Resting on the professor's legs was a book entitled *Historical Outline of the Conquest of the Kingdom of Granada by the Catholic Monarchs, According to the Arabic Chroniclers.*

Majnun felt bad for not knowing how to express what he was thinking, if he was even thinking at all. He finally made an attempt:

"I was hoping to find, within the Islamic tradition, an explanation of tolerance . . ."

He was going to say "of tolerance in relation to the Jews, the co-existence of various religions . . ." but the professor kept on talking in his professorial manner about the era of the Nasrid kings. Majnun, with his mouth half-open, had the expression of someone who was concentrated on his own thoughts. The professor's words sounded like music, animating the images of a time long past, which, for Majnun, continued to be the present. Seeming deep in thought, he saw himself in that remote past, inhaling the cold air that descended from the Sierra Nevada onto the Alhambra, listening to the mysterious silence whose echoes reached into the present like gentle waves, or even watching the battles between Christians and Moors, evoked by the historical cavalry reenactments he'd witnessed in neighboring Pirenópolis. The professor's words troubled him, because they reinforced his conviction that there was something living and sacred in that history that demanded his presence. He again thought about expressing his ideas, so as not to seem ignorant. But what could he say that would reveal any knowledge?

Rodrigo Díaz recounted details of the fall of Granada. He spoke with his long nose inclined forward, looking from side to side with his bulging eyes. Distracted, Majnun missed part of the explanation, but heard the deprecatory remarks about Sultan Abu l-Hassan Ali, also known as Abul Hassan or Muley Hacén.

"It's just like the Prophet Mohammed said, or else it was Caliph Umar: *Kama takounou youalla aleikoum,* or 'You shall have the leaders that you deserve.' Your grandfather told me that you speak Arabic."

"I've been studying it for quite a while. And sometimes I speak it with my grandma Mona, who lives in São Paulo."

"Tolerance, huh?" said the professor.

Is he making light of my interest in the subject? thought Majnun.

"Well then, that sultan," said the professor, continuing, "was the father of the last sultan of Granada, Mohammed XII — or more likely the eleventh, according to recent research — known as Boabdillah or Boabdil, which is how the Spaniards pronounced Abu Abd-Allah or Abu Abdalla. They also called him *El Chico*, or 'the little one.' *Venga*, under Boabdil 'The Unfortunate' there was more tolerance in Granada. For that very reason its inhabitants felt free to criticize him."

"Muslims were more advanced than the Christians. If they hadn't been oppressed, marginalized, humiliated . . ."

"The Christians did end up being even more intolerant, if that's what you're trying to say. You should do some research into it. It would also be worthwhile to compare the Koran and the Old Testament. There's tolerance and intolerance in both of them. So, you're interested in tolerance, is that it?"

How could he respond to that stupid question? But he didn't need to respond, because the professor quickly took up the subject again:

"Voltaire, in his Treatise on Tolerance, called attention to the intolerance in the Bible, where it is said that God once commanded that idolaters be killed. Good thing the Jews didn't kill Catholics using this justification. Moses killed 23,000 men because of the Golden Calf, and in the Book of Numbers it's said that in the war against the Midianites he ordered that all adult males and mothers be killed, and that all spoils be taken. Just a few ideas for your study on intolerance . . ."

"Actually, no. What I want to write about is tolerance in . . ."

"Jews accepted the belief of sacrificing humans to the divinity. What happened was that in practice they sacrificed an expiatory goat, instead of a human being, you understand? And look: Muslims celebrate Abraham's sacrifice every year, because of this decision to save the son and use a lamb instead. In other words, Islam also has ways of avoiding intolerance."

"I read that it says in the Koran that killing a person is like murdering all of humanity."

"Well, killing a person who hasn't committed homicide or sown corruption upon the earth."

Professor Rodrigo, a specialist in Islamic studies, knew many passages from the Koran by heart and quoted them from memory. He spoke with a strong Spanish accent in well-enunciated Portuguese, which Majnun had no trouble understanding.

During the conference—poorly attended, since the university was on break—Majnun sat by himself in one of the last rows, taking notes as best he could on his laptop.

A female professor from the history department—short and thin, with a crooked nose and expressive eyes, who spoke as if she were dancing, shifting her weight back and forth from one foot to the other—introduced the three presenters for the first roundtable of the conference and gave the floor to a French professor.

French? Majnun assumed he'd be blonde, with blue eyes and rosy cheeks. He was black and had almost no cheeks to speak of. He started off by talking about the Arab contributions to European culture during the Middle Ages. One of the birthplaces of Europe was Muslim Toledo. The Arabs, he said, made major contributions in the field of medicine and, along with the Jews, were great surgeons. They made huge gains in astronomy with the perfection and dissemination of the astrolabe. Their architects, who were even contracted to build palaces abroad, invented the transverse arch, situated diagonally in the intrados of the cross vault, which ended up becoming a characteristic of Gothic architecture.

"Let's not forget that Arabic numerals and algebra were both Arabic inventions, which perfected ideas that had come from India," said the French professor. "Another fundamental item: they introduced the use of paper in Europe. This facilitated the circulation of ideas. They brought cotton, rice, sugar cane, palm trees, artichokes, orange, limes . . ."

"Even deodorant and toothpaste," interrupted the professor with the crooked nose, a smile on her face. Majnun didn't know whether or not she was being serious, since the French professor merely nodded in agreement towards her, then continued his lecture without giving any importance to what he'd heard:

"Ultimately, they developed agriculture, manufacturing, and trade," he said. "They established wise and just laws, cultivated the arts, and propagated Eastern wisdom. The Universities of Toledo, Córdoba, Seville, and Granada were sought out by students from many different lands. Madrasas—Islamic schools—were everywhere. Dante, in the *Divine Comedy*, recognized the importance of Islamic culture. He made reference to the Prophet Mohammed, Avicenna, who lived from 980 to 1037, and Averroes, who was born in 1126 and died in 1198."

When the professor mentioned a short story by Borges, "La busca de Averroes"—in which the Arab, who is writing a commentary on Aristotle's *Poetics*, attempts to comprehend the meanings of the words "tragedy" and "comedy"—Majnun immediately thought about appropriating the story for the novella he was writing. He'd download Borges's short story on his computer later.

The Frenchman concluded his lecture by reminding the audience that, if it weren't for the defeats on the plains of Tours, at the edge of the Pyrenees, Muslim rule would have extended throughout all of Europe, to Paris and London even, and to this very day.

A young woman, whose head was covered with a white headscarf and who spoke Portuguese with an accent, asked for the floor. She refuted the fact that Dante had recognized the importance of Islam, since he had put both the Prophet Mohammed and Imam Ali in the ninth valley of the eighth circle of hell, accused of sowing dissidence and discord. Saladin, Avicenna, and Averroes were in the company of the great figures of Greco-Roman thought, but weren't worthy of heaven either. They were all relegated to limbo, said the young woman.

After the controversy had been discussed, a professor from the University of São Paulo, a tall man with an Italian last name and an oval face, who had a nervous habit of scratching the tip of his nose each time he started a sentence, spoke about Jewish contributions to philosophy, poetry, mathematics, medicine, geography, and botany. He dwelled at length on Maimonides, a rabbi, theologian, and doctor who was born in 1135 in Córdoba, died in 1204, and defined the rules according to which scribes began to copy the sacred Jewish texts. With a myopic squint that went back and forth from his papers to the audience, he said that Jews had dedicated themselves to the study of science, translated texts from the Greek and Hebrew into Arabic, and from the Arabic not only into Latin, but also the common languages of the people, and were the most important taxpayers, merchants, and bankers: the vanguard of a nascent capitalism.

He then spoke, scratching the tip of his nose all the while, about the massacres of Jews in Arab Spain, which Professor Rodrigo had mentioned in the car. The situation worsened, he said, with the invasion of the peninsula at the end of the eleventh century by a faction from Morocco called the Almoravids. Expelled in the twelfth century, they were replaced with a more orthodox faction, the Almohads, who persecuted even the Mozarabs, who were Christians living among the Arabs. Jews started to experience greater tolerance when, as a result of the dissolution of the Almohad Empire, the Kingdom of Granada was founded in 1238 by Mohammed I, Ibn al Ahmar, with whom the Nasrid Dynasty and the construction of the Alhambra began. The conference presenter cited the case of Sultan Mohammed V, builder of the Courtyard of the Lions of the Alhambra, who, in 1367, granted refuge in his kingdom to hundreds of Jewish families who would have otherwise fallen into the hands of his enemy, Henry of Trastámara, later known as King Henry II of Castile. At the end of his reign, in 1391, Mohammed V welcomed many refugees who were fleeing the anti-Jewish uproar in Christian territories. Majnun became convinced that he should focus his novella, as well as his essay on tolerance in Islam, on this Nasrid period.

Then he followed the story of the fall of Granada, narrated by Professor Rodrigo Díaz, as if he'd lived through it in the flesh. Majnun visualized the majestic air of Sultan Boabdil, who retained his dignity regardless of the circumstances. He imagined the ambience of the court, the gestures and attire of the people, the argument between those who wanted peace—another name for surrender—and those enemies of the sultan who accused him of not being a true Muslim since he didn't undertake *jihad* against the Catholic monarchs.

That night, he downloaded the Borges story the French professor had alluded to. "Tragedy" and "comedy" were incomprehensible words for Averroes, for they were based on theatrical representation, unknown in the Islamic world. In the story there were, however, occurrences that distracted Averroes, taking him away from his work: some sort of melody, half-naked children playing in a narrow dirt courtyard, live theater. One of the children, standing on the shoulders of another, pretended to be the muezzin, singing, with eyes closed, "There is no god but God." The child holding him, standing still, played the part of the minaret. A third child, kneeling and covered in dust, was the congregation of the faithful. Afterwards, at the home of some friends, Averroes heard a story about a voyage which contained a description of theatrical representation in Sin-Kalan (Canton), but none of the friends understood the necessity of twenty people telling a single story, when, as complex as it may have been, it could be told by just one. Averroes couldn't understand something based on an unknown concept, but there was another notion that was familiar to him: that of the storyteller. Thus, as he took up his manuscript once more, he added: "Aristotle gives the name of 'tragedy' to panegyrics and that of 'comedy' to satires and anathemas. Admirable tragedies and comedies abound in the pages of the Koran . . ." Majnun thought about adding something that he'd found on the internet to this short story: in his commentary on the *Poetics*, Averroes, who had never read the Greek tragedies, saw in the sacrifice of Abraham—an example of an atrocity committed by loved ones—the best illustration of one of the characteristics of tragedy: the capacity to arouse fear and pity simultaneously.

And Majnun's novella? Would it be tragic? Comic? Or written from the perspective of someone who is unfamiliar with the concepts of tragedy and comedy, like Averroes in the Borges story?

He read about the Arab world and the Iberian Peninsula, obsessions of his since he was a child. One subject or historical figure would lead him to others and then others still. From Tunisia he would go to Egypt and to Lebanon. A news item from the present day would recede into the past until it reached the Middle Ages. He followed the Arabs into Spain, witnessing the first modern war in history, for which Granada was unprepared, because it didn't have access to sophisticated armaments like Castile did, not even a single canon.

He spent so many hours in front of his computer that he forgot to eat. He swam so much in the endless sea — the computer screen — that he stayed up all night at times, his eyes red from reading against that gleaming white background, his imagination swelling with impossible causes.

Something strange happened around that time. He had fallen asleep on a bench on the balcony of the house. Then, with his eyes shut, he began to hear steps approaching little by little, footfall after footfall. He felt a presence, someone standing in front of him.

Majnun kept his eyes shut, shuddering out of fear. A rush of air ruffled the sleeve of his shirt, then blew cool against his face. It came from the mouth of the stranger.

He decided to face his fear. He opened his eyes. The man — standing, tall, thin, pale, blonde haired, with light-colored eyes and a majestic bearing — had an intense gaze and calm appearance.

Majnun sat up.

"You called me?"

"Yes, I called you," replied Majnun, recognizing Boabdil.

He couldn't waste this opportunity to ask him some crucial questions:

"I wanted to know the reason behind the war between father and son that ended up weakening Granada."

"In order to consolidate power, my father ordered the decapitation of the Abencerrages, repressed those who criticized him, and, under the influence of his new wife — his former Christian slave, Isabel de Solís, later known as Zoraya — he imprisoned his first wife, Fátima or Aixa, my mother, in the Tower of Comares in the Alhambra. He also imprisoned the two sons he had with her, me and Yusuf.

Zoraya wanted one of her own sons to succeed my father. But the worst is that, to compensate for the opposition he faced for marrying a Christian, he stopped paying the tribute to the Christians. To top it all off, he sent three hundred cavalrymen to take back the Castle of Zahara de la Sierra which had been in the hands of Castile for seventy-five years. Thus began a ten-year war, which was added to a seven-year civil war when, a little less than three months after the taking of the Castle of Zahara, as you know, I escaped from the tower by climbing down a rope and was declared the new sultan in the Albayzín. I had to defend myself against my father's troops stationed in Málaga."

"I understand the circumstances of the surrender," said Majnun.

He recognized that there was very little Boabdil could have done—in the year 896 of the Hijri calendar, with the highways blockaded by the Christians—once the food shortage started in Granada.

"But, Sir, why did you, many years earlier, promise King Fernando that one day you would grant him Granada and sign an agreement to that end in Loja?"

Majnun, sad and indignant, put his head in his hands.

"I had no choice. The Christians had taken me prisoner. And they had my two sons, Ahmed and Yusuf, as hostages and only released them more than a year after my surrender."

"And why didn't the Mameluk sultan in Egypt, the Turks, or the Maghrebis come to your aid?"

Boabdil didn't respond. The luminosity that emanated from his body began to grow dim.

"Why didn't Granada invest in canons? Why did you just passively watch while the Christians rapidly built—with stones from the old Moorish buildings—the walls of Santa Fé, right there close to you?" Majnun screamed, so that Boabdil, who was disappearing, could still hear him.

Boabdil disappeared into the bright of day when Dario, cigar in hand, came out and scolded his grandson for having spent the night on the balcony.

"Sir, do you think he was right not to want any canons, any more death?" Majnun asked his grandfather.

"You're dreaming. Go to bed."

It hadn't been a dream, he thought. After all, Boabdil had disappeared during a battle in Morocco after the fall of Granada. He was a sort of Dom Sebastian, lost in battle. He could return.

Gazes attempting to interpret each other

A month after Professor Rodrigo's visit, Majnun went out with Carmen to a bar in the Asa Norte area near the University of Brasilia. It was February of 2011. Carmen knew too much about him. She was either very astute or had spoken with Suzana. He couldn't stand Suzana. He didn't know why he had spent an entire afternoon talking with her poolside at the Cota Mil Athletic Club, and then a long night finishing up that conversation during a party at her apartment, revealing much more to her than he should have. Or he knew quite well. It wasn't because he was interested in what he was hearing, but because he was interested in what he was seeing. He got nothing out of kilometers worth of her words, but he didn't miss a single millimeter of her thighs. His ears, serious and critical, wanted to call it quits. But his easygoing eyes wanted to stay. They liked vulgarity, that was the reason. In the apartment, hypnotized by the low neckline that precisely revealed the volume of her tightly pushed-up breasts and promised an ample view down towards her stomach, those eyes took his other senses hostage to an emotion that was unjustified, but real: that of discovery.

Carmen knew intimate things about him, which he hadn't mentioned to Suzana or anyone else. Who could have told her about Laila? Well, it's true that she hadn't said the name "Laila," she'd merely asked after his girlfriend, wondering if she was in Brasilia ... But right at the time when Laila was traveling throughout Europe with her husband. How did she know about him spending hours on end on social media, since he never used his real name on there? How did she find out that he had submitted a short story to a contest?

"My life is made up of doubts," said Majnun. "I don't know what I want to be, I can't find a job ... I spend my afternoons alone, dedicated to my inner world or on Twitter and Facebook."

"You prefer solitude, you're a misanthrope."

"Solitude is misanthropy? Me, a misanthropist? Don't I go out to clubs? To parties? You even met me at a party. But I have to admit, I don't like commitments. I don't even have my friends' phone numbers."

"Guy friends?"

Might she be insinuating that he was gay?

"I always prefer women. If they're insensitive, cold, violent, crude, bossy, or bowlegged, then they're just poorly formed men. I have to confess that, for the first time, I'm in love," he said, referring to Laila without using her name. "My girlfriend is traveling," he added. "I don't know when she's coming back, but she promised me our separation would be brief."

The conversation grew to such a point that, after three beers, Carmen recounted — without remorse and in a good-humored manner — her sad story, which even included the tale of her brother, murdered by twelve blows from a machete, and her adventures as a street kid. Her mother, from a poor family in the Northeast, had gotten pregnant as an adolescent by a man who never even lived with her.

"I was born to a virgin mother; my father ejaculated on her thighs. I was literally created on a laptop," she said, a smile widening on her refined face, full of charm, wrinkles appearing at the corners of her eyes.

How old was Carmen? Maybe twenty-eight. Or at most thirty. Her hairstyle, worn up, suited her curly hair, which was so black it looked like a dye-job. Her breasts — well hidden in her blouse, which went up to her neck — couldn't quite hide their youthful firmness. Her baggy pants didn't reveal the outline of her body. Her white blouse was also baggy, with sleeves down to her wrists, which made no sense in that heat. And, yet, Majnun found intense grace in that studied inelegance.

"In my veins flows the Iberian blood of my grandfather Sérgio mixed with the Arab blood of my grandmother Mona. His family moved from Asturias to Portugal in the sixteenth century, then took up residence in northeastern Brazil in the seventeenth century. So I'm also half-northeasterner. But grandpa Sérgio was born and raised in São Paulo. In 1975, on a flight to Beirut, where he was headed as a reporter, he couldn't take his eyes off of the girl beside him. He himself will tell you: what he noticed were her long fingers, her perfect nose, and her thin ankles. I think the fact that she was a visual artist also swayed my grandpa Sérgio, as well as her curious personal history: she's the daughter of an Egyptian mother and a Palestinian-Lebanese father. Their day-to-day life was dangerous; every time one of my grandparents wanted to visit the other they had to pass through various check-points. She lived on a little lane close to Hamra Street in an area controlled by the Lebanese National Movement, a coalition of parties under Druze leadership, and he lived in Jounieh, by the sea, in a Christian region. One time when he visited her, he had to stay for two days, unable to return home. The consequence: she got pregnant, they got married, and my father was born."

From which one can conclude, let's say, at this point, that misfortunes can be the origin of joys as well as—as it will be possible to deduce from the remainder of the story—the origin of further misfortunes.

"My grandparents Mona and Sérgio lived together in Lebanon until 1982, when he capped off the experience with articles on the suppressed insurrection of the armed branch of the Muslim Brotherhood in Hama, Syria, and the Israeli invasion of Lebanon. These days he covers the Middle East for the Estado de São Paulo newspaper."

"So these São Paulo grandparents are your favorites."

"I admire them all, my grandparents here in Brasilia as well, my maternal grandparents."

He thought about saying that, out of all them, the one he liked least was his grandpa Sérgio, but no, this had no bearing on the subject.

"I admire the lives they lived," he continued, "completely different from the grandeur-free times we live in. My grandpa Dario, the one who lives here in Brasilia, studied in a Dominican seminary. He left there to study law and take up militant politics. He was hounded by the dictatorship, interrogated by the Department of Political and Social Order, fled Brazil, and lived in Paris from the beginning of the seventies until 1985. That is, he stayed in Paris for six years after the amnesty, perfecting his law studies. As he likes to say, he didn't trust the transition process. He retained some monkish qualities from his religious upbringing. He transformed into an atheist who could give political sermons. In Paris, he met my grandma Elvira—quite a bit younger than him—who was finishing a dissertation on sewage engineering. In 1975, she gave him a daughter: my mom."

"What an interesting character, this grandpa Dario of yours!"

"He always fought for justice. When he returned to Brazil, he rose in rank by his own merits and retired as a judge. I admire his courage, his unselfishness, his political activism. To me, he is the person of greatest character in our entire family. I don't agree with him on everything, but I'll always listen to what he has to say."

Majnun sometimes watched him in silence, a silence filled with pride. The affection that united them awoke a desire in the grandson to learn from Dario, to emulate his experience, to be a modern version of what his grandfather was, fully developing the tendencies he'd been born with, which were also, in large part, inherited.

"Our problem these days is the era we live in, an era without the challenges that grandpa Dario had to face, don't you think?"

What caught his attention most about Carmen were her unkempt, bitten nails, the slender nude body he imagined underneath those baggy pants, her large, dark eyes, and her angular face; the contrast of firmness and tenderness in her gait, now that she had walked over to use the restroom.

Majnun looked at her profile, head held high, one hand in her pocket—like a man—and the other on the nape of her neck, like a runway model. Although she was of average height, she was taller than him. In her flats, she strode as if walking on feathers, cotton. Majnun didn't miss a single detail of her stroll down the runway.

When she returned, he looked into Carmen's eyes. Affectionate, sincere eyes. He looked at her hands. Delicate hands, even without the benefit of a manicure.

Carmen returned his gaze without shyness. And there was a silence between these two gazes, which attempted to interpret each other. Was it possible to love two women at the same time, for him, who had never had sex with a single one, not even with Laila? Laila had showered him with affection and promises, while still imposing her limits. And then left on her trip.

Satan makes indecent proposals here as well

The jealousy Majnun felt for Laila was nearly driving him mad. For the first time he understood the pain of absence, which became imbued with fear when he received an old-school postcard from Laila, a reproduction of an 1847 painting by the Belgian artist Antoine Wiertz, on display in the Brussels Museum of Modern Art: *La belle Rosine*, a nude woman contemplating a skeleton.

How to interpret Laila's interest in this painting? Save for the color of her skin, which was darker than Laila's, the woman resembled Laila herself: thick thighs, large backside, ample breasts, a thick neck that supported a face with a long, refined nose, thin eyebrows, and an engaged look in her eyes. With her right hand she held the end of a diaphanous sheet; with her left, a ring on one of the fingers, she grasped a red sheet, both of the sheets falling down around the middle of her thighs. He read the complete title of the painting: *Deux jeunes filles ou la belle Rosine*. There was a tragic note in the contemplation of that other *jeune fille*, who was even taller and was nothing more than a skeleton, with neither arms nor legs. He noticed the tag on the skeleton's skull. "La belle Rosine" was written there. Therefore, the skeleton belonged to the beautiful woman, whose beauty was fleeting, like life itself. Certainly, she had been admired, vain, and prideful of her body. Majnun thought of Suzana, but soon dismissed that macabre thought, which wasn't even really a thought, just an intrusive image. Then he inverted the images: the young woman who contemplated the skeleton had the skin color of Suzana, and could well be her. The skeleton, then, was Laila? The idea provoked a chill in his stomach, which increased when he saw a sculpture of a head on the ground below the skeleton, behind another sculpture still, of a foot. He then recalled the dream in which he, Majnun, was just a head. He tried to calm himself down. Ultimately, it was nothing more than a postcard, an antiquated object that was going out of use more and more each day.

A few days later, Majnun was shopping with Laila in Beverly

Hills. After that, in New York, he had lunch with her at Le Cirque, then walked down 59th Street to Central Park and strolled among the golden, autumnal trees. They visited a gallery in SoHo to buy a painting by Gerhard Richter. They soon found themselves in Paris drinking a kir at *Deux Magots*, then stopped by the Louvre to admire *Le Tricheur à l'as de carreau* by Georges de La Tour. At the Tour d'Argent restaurant they drank a Chateau Lafite Rothschild Pauillac. In London they got calluses from walking two kilometers along the banks of the Thames on a cold, ashen day. They listened, in awe, to the Royal Philharmonic playing Mahler's Fifth at the Royal Festival Hall in the Southbank Centre. They saw a performance of *King Lear*, put on by the Royal Shakespeare Company. Lastly, in Rome, they had drinks at the Antico Caffè Greco, on the Via dei Condotti, near the Piazza di Spagna.

Majnun had never felt so free. Free to imagine, imagining himself traveling with Laila around the world. This was his version of freedom. He traveled around the world without knowing anything of it, save for São Paulo and the Central Plain region in which he lived. The world was that which he read in history books and, above all, what he saw on the internet. From city to city, country to country, he witnessed atrocities: crime, violence, misery, hunger, environmental disasters . . . From one hour to the next he didn't know where he was, which city he was in, which country. Was he in a hospital or an asylum? What language were they speaking all around him? Like a drunk. A drug addict. Like when he claimed that he wasn't a Brazilian, but an Egyptian named Ibrahim bin Ayyub. At which point his grandma Elvira threatened to take him to the doctor.

Captive in his chair, he felt free to imagine, to lie. Since the tickets were free, he always traveled quickly, in comfort, with no turbulence, delays, or canceled flights. He went from one continent to another with Laila in a fraction of a second. But he had to recognize that he was captive in that place, that bedroom, that chair, at that computer.

In the wee hours that night, in front of the computer screen which illuminated his face, no one was interested in his adventures in foreign lands. No one except for Ava Gardner, who wanted to meet him. But who was this Ava Gardner, aside from the deceased actress who was distracting his attention from Laila and his reflections about the future?

Might he live somewhere with Laila? Would he one day have a profession? The computer kept him company. His passion for history saved him. But, he recognized, he was no genius and had problems with concentration. How else could he explain the fact that he almost had to repeat a year in school and was unable to pass a middling college-entrance exam? Maybe it was for the best. If he had passed, what future would have been waiting for him? It wouldn't be his success, but his failure that would fill his baggage with information and experience, and lead him, after a period of uncertainty, to participate in grand events. To stride towards his great destiny. Was that expecting too much of his future?

His failure wasn't his alone, he then thought; it was also the failure of a turbulent era which had no clear path. If the objectives and hopes of the era in which he lived were at fault, it was necessary to make a heroic gesture: to construct the past and the future with independence and boldness. Yes, even the past. He could do this by writing his novella.

Of course, his life would be incomplete without a job. But just any job? A sacrifice made in exchange for survival? He was unable to imagine a job that wouldn't sidetrack him from his desires and interests, alienate him from that which he held dear, exhaust his creative energies. Idleness was better, the luxury of time without clocks.

He was definitely unaccustomed to discipline. At school, when they asked him to solve a problem or analyze a question, he got lost in digressions and divagations, although nobody surpassed him when it came to inventing or — in the words of his detractors — lying. He would have had to do his military service, but a doctor friend of his grandpa Dario, knowing of his plans to prepare for the history entrance exams in São Paulo at the University of Campinas, was able to get him on the excess quota list. His head, swirling like the hurricane on Saturn, became even more stuffed with fantasies, random thoughts, stories read and imagined.

In the recesses of his mind, he was able to create a new world and precisely reconstruct the most distant past, even an unknown past, which could lead him to the most revolutionary or reactionary extremes. He saw himself as a radical, a destroyer, or an inventor, capable of reestablishing traditions or shattering them. He could end up—who knows?—a man of action like his grandpa Dario.

Political militant? Not the way they used to be in his grandparents' day. There was no longer a dictatorship to fight against, and it wasn't enough just to join forces with mediocrity, merely adding another cog to the machine, righting an injustice here and there, doing the work of an ant, filling a hole, fixing a defect. His grandma Elvira worked on projects like that for city hall. But he had never been able to be practical. He could try his hand at painting, like his other grandma, Mona. But to what end, if he lacked talent?

For now, the future didn't shine bright in his black eyes. At the age of twenty, he was just a blank canvas. Once again examining the postcard that Laila had sent him, he noticed an easel on the right-hand side of the painting that bore the inscription:

Ebauche
faire bien n'est
qu'une question de temps.

He would have to wait.

Live as much as you can

One night, still in February 2011, the conversations were many and varied around the large dining room table. His grandparents had invited a couple to dinner; a professor of sociology from the University of Brasilia, now retired, an old friend of his grandmother, and her husband, a doctor who, despite his age, still dedicated himself to his pediatric clinic. In addition to their wrinkles and white hair, they had in common the fact that they'd lived in Paris as students. If I could, thought Majnun, I'd relive the lives of my grandparents in the sixties and seventies, either in Paris or the Middle East.

The appetizer having just been served — a vichyssoise — the subject turned to the Spanish professor who had recently been in Brasilia.

"I met him when we lived in Paris in the early seventies," clarified grandpa Dario. "He was already interested in Islamic studies and medieval Spain back then."

"I wish I had lived in the sixties . . . or seventies," said Majnun.

His desire was genuine, not only because of the envy he felt for the time his maternal grandparents had spent in Paris, but also because of everything he'd heard over the years from his paternal grandparents, who had met in Beirut. Every one of them had a story to tell about an era of major events. And what about him? Would he someday take part in a major event?

Dario pulled from his goatee recollections long kept under lock and key. The most precious of them had to do with his friendship with Rodrigo, the Spanish professor, who was then a student like him. Not yet dating Elvira, he had traveled to Spain, and Rodrigo had given him the number of a friend in Barcelona. Dario would never forget Alicia kissing him on the mouth in the middle of Park Güell, nor the hours spent with her in his hotel room. She later told him, "for the love of God, don't say anything to Rodrigo." Which is when Dario realized that the charming Spaniard was more than just a friend to Rodrigo. Dario's old friend only let on that he knew of that encounter years after his marriage to Alicia and her untimely death from cancer. Despite—or because of—the conversation that juxtaposed the resentment of one against the apologies of the other, their friendship continued.

"You shouldn't wish to live through the things we lived through, my son," was the response that Majnun received from his grandma Elvira, who on this night had tastefully applied makeup and whose elegance was accentuated by her green dress and string of costume-jewelry pearls. "In Brazil, we had the dictatorship. In France, young people thought they were going to change the world. The end of hierarchy, the challenge to authority . . . And do you know what came of it?"

"A lot," said Dario, jumping in. "It was a breach in the wall, as we used to say. A change of mentality, in the relationships between men and women, parents and children, a greater attention paid to ecology . . ."

"But starting in the eighties there was a conservative reaction," recalled Elvira.

"After the French Revolution came the Restoration, but that doesn't mean the revolution was just a useless detour," defended Dario.

"The French Revolution? Ah, there was no French Revolution," protested his grandmother, chuckling. "And what do you all think?" she asked the invited couple, who accompanied the discussion with slight movements of their heads, as if they were watching a ping-pong match.

Majnun hadn't imagined that he would provoke such an animated discussion between his grandparents. A breach in the wall? If only such a thing were possible in Brazil.

"The students' wild democracy liberated the imagination. Against compromise, against convention . . ." said Dario.

"And what was the result?" demanded Elvira, with a touch of irritation.

"Well, a lot of taboos died out. New ideas entered the culture. The spirit of the times changed. Society transformed into something else, developed a different sensibility," Dario insisted, looking towards their friends, who were still mutely following the ping-pong ball.

Majnun was immersed in anxieties about his destiny.

"There's no denying it, Elvira. It was a party, an explosion of joy. I've read that even psychosomatic illnesses disappeared, but on the other hand . . ." said the doctor hesitatingly, quickly interrupted by his wife:

"It's forbidden to forbid, as they said around these parts. In praise of desire, of pleasure . . . Desire this, desire that. Everything was about desire, no?"

"You know what was unleashed by May of 1968? An increase in the sale of pornography," said Elvira sarcastically.

"No, don't confuse the issue. My friends, May of '68 has nothing to do with hedonist individualism, which only began in the middle of the seventies and, justly, corresponded with the failure of the ideals of May of '68," said Dario, meeting the gaze of each of those present and emphasizing his phrases with a movement of his index finger.

"Oh, good! So you admit that they failed," rejoined Elvira, her hands straightening up her short hair.

"What we can't do is lose the sense of the more general meaning of the movement. The aspirations of women and other minorities . . ." the doctor began to argue, looking upward, as if searching for inspiration.

"Women are a minority?" interrupted Elvira, but he kept on speaking, talking in a clear, deliberate manner, as if he hadn't heard her:

"The search for truth and justice, the attempts at communal living, the rediscovery of brotherhood, of solidarity, the flag of autonomy and self-management . . . Then came the hippies, who opposed the culture of consumerism. All of this found its place . . . And it was a peaceful revolution. Without the use of weapons."

"Oh, my dear, forgive me, but you're confusing one thing for another," said Elvira in disagreement.

"Well, you're right about *that*, it wasn't a single thing. The youth movement had many faces," said Dario. "There was also a militant

Marxist nucleus. That's where the Trotskyites and Maoists were."

"And there was, in a second-wave movement, a general workers' strike. With precise, limited reassertions," added the professor.

"Many of the Trotskyites turned into neo-hippies," concluded Elvira.

"But the greater ambition was youth's desire to transform society," argued the doctor. "Nanterre was merely the fuse. The movement soon spread. And there were, of course, similar movements in other countries. At Berkeley, the London School of Economics . . . And let's not forget the counterculture, the civil rights movement in the United States . . ."

"Or the Prague Spring," said the professor.

"Let's not mix things up here. That was a phenomenon of a different nature entirely, with a clear political meaning," said Dario.

"The uprising in France was a fight against abstract monsters: the sys-tem, so-ci-ety, po-wer . . ." said Elvira, emphasizing each syllable.

"What I find interesting is that it all took place at a time when there was no economic crisis," said the professor, trying to take the conversation in another direction, with an argument similar to some of those made about Chile in 2011, and Brazil and Turkey when 2013 rolled around. "When the economic crisis did come, in 1973, the movement began to weaken," continued the professor. "Dissatisfaction with alienating labor became less important than simply finding a job . . . Survival always takes precedence . . ."

At that point, Dario, looking at Majnun, asserted:

"You can't go back in time, of that you can be certain. Live as much as you can while you are young, so you don't regret it later. It doesn't matter if you make mistakes. Mistakes are a part of life. Be free, even when freedom is just a chimera. It isn't worth it to be so realistic that you end up settled down and indifferent."

For Majnun, it was as if his grandpa knew about his affair with Laila and was absolving him of his mistake. Those words spoke to a hidden, essential part of his soul where Laila lay dormant—that is, if he even had a soul and if Laila ever slept. But of course not, he didn't have a soul and Laila was never dormant. On the contrary, she occupied his thoughts, all of his being, waking him up, caressing him, leaving him perpetually without peace.

"I'm old. Getting old means accumulating losses and living on memories. You know what? My best memories are those of my freedom," concluded Dario, much to Majnun's delight.

He was now certain of it: his grandfather was talking about Laila. She was set to arrive, and Majnun was going to welcome her with an alleviated conscience.

However, his alleviated conscience didn't impede the arrival of Boabdil, the Sultan of Granada, who, that night, again appeared to him, this time dressed in white and without the vestments of a sultan.

"I am Ibrahim," Majnun told him.

The sultan didn't believe him and decided that he would be executed.

Majnun searched around for the chessboard, on which, as he moved the pieces, he would be able to provoke internal wars among Granada's enemies and protect it from the Christian invasion. He found only his iPad and couldn't turn it on. Boabdil then ordered two strong men to take him to the scaffold. Majnun kicked his legs, lacking the strength to escape.

He awoke, panting, at the very moment he was to be executed. His body was bathed in a cold sweat. There was no doubt this time: it was a dream. What a relief!

There was an explanation for the presence of Ibrahim in the dream. A long time ago he had read in a book from his grandfather's library, written by Washington Irving, the legend of Ibrahim bin Ayyub, the Arab astrologer and doctor who arrived on foot at the court of the Moorish Sultan Aben Habuz in Granada, having traveled from Egypt. Majnun had almost been forced by his grandma to see a doctor, precisely because he insisted that his name was Ibrahim. And, more recently, as he was writing the first version of his novella as a short story to submit to a contest, he imagined he was Ibrahim, transforming himself into the main character.

Upon her return, Laila arranged to pick him up in her car at the exit of CasaPark in the middle of the afternoon. She arrived driving a black Land Rover and was unrecognizable in sunglasses, a black dress, and a black scarf around her head, like an orthodox Muslim. Upon seeing so much black, Majnun had a bad premonition. As soon as he got in the car, she warned him:

"My husband read one of your emails. He hit me, wanting to know who you were and threatened me, saying: 'I'm going to kill you if you leave me.' He's looking for you and is going to kill you. And he's capable of it too, I know him very well."

"I'm going to buy bullets for my revolver."

"I think it's better for us to stop seeing each other."

"Why? Because I'm going to buy bullets?"

"Don't do such a crazy thing, my God."

"You're not going to tell me you're afraid of your husband, are you?" he said, unable to mask his frustration.

"Shouldn't I be?"

"I'm going to report that son of a bitch to the police," he said angrily, raising his voice.

"No, don't even think about it."

Her green eyes filled with tears. The tears dissolved Majnun's anger, and he pulled Laila towards him, resting her head on his shoulder.

"I can take money out of the joint savings account I have together with my grandparents. It's enough for us to live on for half a year. Let's go to the Northeast."

"Money isn't the problem. My store makes enough money. But . . . no, forget about it."

"And why not? Just because you're afraid?" he said, getting heated again.

Right there in the middle of the highway, he sucked gluttonously on her ample breasts, his nervous hands on Laila's supple thighs. She then suggested:

"Don't get the idea that I'm accustomed to this sort of thing, but I've heard about this motel, Paradise of Love."

He was the one that wasn't accustomed to anything. But he could make it look like it wasn't his first time. She showed him the bruises on her body, the result of her husband's blows; and he showed her a discreet tattoo high up on his thigh, with the words "eternal love." On that long afternoon, which turned into evening, he found her joyful one minute, frightened the next. To cap off their tryst, he removed from his pocket a cigar that he had stolen from his grandpa Dario. He took a drag and said:

"We aren't going to deprive ourselves of the best things in life. We have to keep seeing each other. A day without you is a day that doesn't even count at all."

"I love you, I'll always love you. And I don't love my husband. I think I never really loved him. But I realize that we're living a dream here. This isn't really happening. We have to wake up," she said with a somber air, but her face was offered to him, her breasts offered, her entire body offered, and he immediately attended to that offering with kisses on her hands, her face, her breasts, her stomach, her sex, her thighs.

She got up, pale, with a tragic countenance and downturned lips. She paced through the room to the beat of the elevator-music bossa nova on the radio.

Majnun saw something sad in the slow gait of that beautiful, naked body. And he was saddened.

Awake from your dream

A few days later, Mona and Sergio, his grandparents from São Paulo, arrived. Mona was taking part in a collective exhibition at the National Museum.

It was February 2011. On that morning Majnun hurriedly greeted his grandparents, freshly arrived from São Paulo, then holed up in his bedroom. Ever since they had said goodbye, Laila hadn't replied to his emails or answered calls to her cell phone. Why did he have to scare her by saying he was going to buy bullets? He understood Laila. She preferred, logically, not to love a dead man.

He sent out a tweet: "it's enough to have a single moment swift as lightning that sums up all of life, a radical moment described with definitive words."

Would Laila respond? He tore off a scrap of paper and wrote the same phrase in pencil. He tossed the scrap into a shoebox, half-full of scribbled pages, receipts, napkins, pieces torn from notepads, and bits of paper. Always a phrase randomly scribbled down, as if he were Fernando Pessoa making notes for his *Book of Disquiet*. Sometimes he'd choose a phrase at random out of the box, like fortune cookies at a Chinese restaurant.

There were also pages strewn about the desk, the novella that he had mentioned to the Spanish professor and continued writing and rewriting, still seeing himself as Ibrahim bin Ayyub, son of a contemporary of the Prophet Mohammed. He reread the legend of that Arab astrologer and doctor who had become a counselor to Sultan Aben Habuz of Granada after inventing a mechanical instrument made of forged bronze, in the shape of a ram and a rooster. Any time the country was threatened by an invasion, the ram turned towards the direction of the enemy and the rooster crowed. The astrologer was the holder of the *Book of Wisdom*, which was discovered along with the mummy of a high priest in a burial chamber in the center of a pyramid in Egypt, the book given to Adam when he left paradise and which had been passed down from generation to generation to King

Solomon the Wise. With the knowledge from this book, he built a tower, on top of which was a circular room with windows facing each of the cardinal directions. Set in front of each window was a table which displayed, as on a chessboard, wooden figures representing the armies of the monarchs who ruled kingdoms in those directions. On each of these tables was also a small spear, used to touch the wooden figures and thus destabilize and foment internal conflicts among his enemies. At the top of the tower, a bronze cavalryman, also armed with a spear, revealed approaching danger by turning towards the direction of the advancing enemy.

Majnun was going to transport the legend to a precise historical era. He would exercise his magical powers on the death rattle of Muslim dominion in order to save it from the Christian invasion, which had caused so much calamity in the world.

A new spring started during spring itself

Lunch was served out on the balcony where Majnun ate breakfast with his grandpa Dario—the four grandparents, plus him, Majnun, were reunited around the cast-iron table.

Sérgio—fat, tall, completely bald—was sipping a *jerez* as an aperitif. He always drank *jerez*, not *arak*, to remember Lebanon through that mystery of sensations which allows them to travel back to specific places and moments. He had acquired the habit of drinking *jerez* with a Lebanese friend—a Maronite Christian—before big lunches during which they ate heavily seasoned lamb.

"I read your article, Sérgio. Are you sticking your nose into domestic politics?" asked Dario, adding that because of his article, he and Elvira had decided to reread *Quincas Borba*.

Sérgio usually only wrote about the Middle East, but in one piece he had included a quote from a character in Machado's novel: "'They can do whatever they wish,' said the doctrinaire, 'but moral punishment is certain. The debts of each party will be paid with interest down to the last cent and the final generation. Principles do not die; the parties who forget them breathe their last breath in the mire, in ignominy.'"

"Look, I'm against those who put leaders ahead of the cause and prefer results to the rule of law," said Sérgio, emphatically.

Majnun thought he was a snob. He didn't feel the same admiration for him that he felt for his grandpa Dario. He recognized that Sérgio knew a few things and he was going to take advantage of his visit to learn about the Middle East. Might he know something about tolerance in Islam?

The food was served: three *picanha* cuts of beef cooked on the grill, toasted manioc flour, and rice.

As the years passed, Mona's physical beauty, which Majnun knew of from photographs, had been preserved in her dark skin and her black, expressive eyes. Since she had grown fatter, she looked shorter than she did in the old photographs, and even her eyes were hidden behind thick-framed glasses. Mona looked out onto the garden, where the gardener was working under the intense sun:

"Your garden is well maintained," she said in her agreeable manner.

"And Tunisia, huh? What do you think is going to happen there?" Dario asked Sérgio, a glass of beer in front of him.

"An Islamic party is going to rise to power," interjected Elvira, taking a sip of her *caipirinha*.

Mona said nothing, but she wrinkled up her brow, as if to ask: "so what?" She was the only one who didn't drink alcohol.

"Some time ago we were talking about the youth movement in Paris in '68. It was spontaneous, it wasn't organized by a party or a union, it took the whole world by surprise, it was an affront to power, and it paralyzed the nation for an entire month. A little like what's happening now in Tunisia," said Dario.

"It's got nothing to do with it. This time the revolution might really take hold. Tunisia has proved that dictatorships can fall in a matter of weeks," argued Sérgio.

Majnun didn't like it when he spoke louder than the rest, as if trying to impose his arguments by way of decibels.

Silent, they all waited for him to continue speaking in his authoritative voice:

"On the other hand, the Muslim Brotherhood and even the Salafists could rise to power democratically. They could impose sharia and curtail the liberties of women. It's like when the communist parties were running in Europe, a liberal regime coexisting with opposing ideologies, the scorpion biting its own tail."

"Holy Mary! According to sharia, a husband has the right to beat his wife," said Elvira, up in arms. "When inheritances are divided up, women only get half as much as men. They can't be leaders. And they're obligated to wear that stupid veil."

"In secular states, like Turkey and others, domestic violence is a crime," Mona explained calmly.

"True. In those cases, the law isn't based in sharia," added Sérgio.

"There's no such thing as a secular Muslim country. Maybe

Turkey, Egypt, and Tunisia . . . who knows, perhaps Morocco. They still practice polygamy, repudiation, or marriage with prepubescent girls based only on the consent of the father," retorted Elvira, still worked-up.

She looked around, adjusted herself in the chair, took another sip of her *caipirinha*, and continued:

"Look here: for a man, divorce is the easiest thing in the world. But for a woman, it depends on such difficult conditions that she ends up back in her parents' home, waiting for her husband to repudiate her. In some countries, an adulterous woman can be killed. And there's no way a betrayed woman could have this right to kill: even if the husband already has four wives, if a wife catches him in the act with someone else, he can always say that he has just then repudiated her, and marry the new lover."

Elvira crossed and uncrossed her legs, then continued:

"When it's said that a state is Islamic, that Islam is the state religion, or that Sharia is one of the sources of the law, you shouldn't trust it: it means that there is no equality between men and women."

"No, not in Tunisia. Even during the dictatorship, the constitution dictated freedom of conscience and the equality of all citizens," said Sergio, clarifying.

"It's based on the Koran, which states that in the beginning human beings were all part of one community, and that Allah created males and females and divided people into different races and tribes. It doesn't say that man holds the highest honor, but, rather, whoever is the most fearful before God," added Mona.

Majnun followed the conversation, trying to extract some lesson out of it that he could use in his essay about tolerance in Islam, which he was going to include in his novella, but his grandma Elvira's opinions left him disheartened.

"Religious dictatorships are the worst," she said in her strong Pernambucan accent, "because they want to control more than just politics. They want to control people's private lives. And these radical Islamists? One thing's for sure: they're afraid of women. I'm against all religious radicals, including the Christian ones. Look at the Christian right in the USA: they claim to be pro-life in the case of abortion, yet they're in favor of the death penalty. It's a contradiction. Those fanatics even make violent attacks on the clinics. And then argue that if abortions were performed in the past, Beethoven wouldn't have been born. Look, by that logic, no one could ever refuse a fuck!"

"The fundamentalists especially want the Sunnah to be enforced," said Sérgio, nursing a beer.

"The active ignorance of the fanatics," said Dario.

"But you became a fanatic on the opposite extreme with your militant atheism," said Elvira.

"No, I'm not a fanatic. Fanaticism is rooted in faith, which is a social ill since it doesn't require justification or tolerate argumentation, as I recently read in an excellent book. My only weapons are words. I'm not going to set off a bomb as a way of defending my arguments."

"Believers are happier than skeptics," said Mona.

"A drunken man is happier than a sober one, as George Bernard Shaw, I think, once reminded us."

"The Sunnah," said Sérgio, to clarify, picking up his explanation and his beer once again, "is the behavior of the Prophet, mainly recorded in *hadith*, which relate what was said or done by the Prophet and his companions. The ulama distinguish between the reliable *hadiths* and the less reliable ones. There are those who accept fifty thousand of them and others who only accept seventeen."

"I don't understand Islam or Islamic law the way you do, but it's clear to me that the application of this, in legal terms, would be an enormous setback," said Dario.

"The application of sharia law would be a horror. Those radical Muslims measure the chastity of women by the centimeter. That's not Islam, it's tribal culture. You must agree with me," said Elvira, turning to Mona, "because you don't adhere to that craziness. There's no such thing as freedom when you mix religion and state. Religion is a curse, and always dominated by men."

"Don't generalize," said Dario.

"I know, I know. There are exceptions: Greek mythology, African religions . . . But that doesn't invalidate my point. In general, religion isn't good for anything except creating feelings of guilt, rivalries, and discrimination—against women, against gays . . . It has only led to disaster. Contrary to art and reason, which unite people, religion divides people."

"Just to clarify: together with the Koran, the Sunnah is the basis of sharia, which is Islamic law," said Mona, politely.

"True. As long as they don't understand that the Koran is a cultural and historical product," argued Dario.

"And now they're switching from suicide to revolution," added Elvira.

"The youth of the revolution are moderate and democratic," posited Mona in a soft voice, as if apologizing for having spoken.

"I doubt it. Only time will tell," objected Elvira, firmly.

"These days all it takes is communication to get people out into the streets. In Tunisia the crowds gathered on Bourguiba Avenue. People filled the avenue, from the old theater to the clock tower in the roundabout. Two days later, the Al-Kitab bookstore was already able to put formerly banned books in the window displays," informed Sérgio.

"An explosion of enthusiasm on the internet amplifies the event, but it's not a revolution, Sérgio. Will alone isn't enough," affirmed Elvira.

Majnun, who spent a large part of his time in front of the computer, asked himself what would happen in Brazil if information started to circulate that would get people out into the streets. Nothing, absolutely nothing, he concluded. Only carnival and soccer mobilized people. His generation demanded change and was indignant, just not in this country. The revolution was starting in the Middle East. Indignation, in Spain. He knew the verses of the Syrian poet Adonis entitled "The Dream and the Awaking":

> *Create in your dream*
> *a model of rebellious revolution*
> *which embraces the growing future.*

Awake from your dream
and your days transform
into wistfulness
which mourns the night that has passed
and its lost chimera.

"Look, there's no other way. It's necessary to defeat oppression with democracy, not more oppression," defended Mona.

Her opinion was respected by all, with the exception of Elvira, who didn't tolerate authoritative arguments, no matter where they came from. Mona was the only Arab and the only Muslim at the table. The only one who had been born in the Middle East, a Palestinian of Egyptian and Lebanese descent.

"What do you know? You've lived here for almost thirty years and have already become Brazilianized," said Elvira, addressing Mona.

"All I know is that it's a good thing that conflicts which were once concealed are now coming to the surface," said Mona, without responding to the provocation.

"Once you destroy order, how do you suddenly create a new order? If everything is destroyed, it's more likely that the new order will impose itself by force. Those who want an end to the chaos may seek solutions from Islamist or nationalist ideologies. Or worse, a dictatorship takes clear control. No, I don't know. At the very least you could end up with the opposite of a democracy: fundamentalism is liberated, majority populations end up being sectarian. Traditional forces could prevail, and the youth on social media would remain on the margins of it all, don't you think?" said Dario, addressing Sérgio.

"It's true, I must confess. I'm not saying that it's going to happen, but in fact they could end up regressing when it comes to religious freedom and women's rights," said Sérgio, reinforcing the argument. "The Salafists want to impose Sharia law, persecute women who don't wear the *niqab*; and moderate Islam, which is coming to power, may tolerate the Salafists. Liberty doesn't just liberate good things. It also liberates backwardness, prejudices, and animosities. But, if you continue to have liberty, space also emerges for changes in other directions, including the best directions. What I want to say is that conflicts are inevitable, but, with time, reason wins out."

"Are you a Kantian?" asked Dario.

"I know," continued Sérgio, "it's going to take a while for the Arab world to rediscover its best tradition, the tradition of its greatness and tolerance. And a wholly democratic secular government, which would even allow a Muslim to be governed by a non-Muslim . . ."

Turning to Majnun, he added:

"Maybe you'll witness that one day; not me."

"About women, I just want to say one thing: at a time when even the United States hasn't had a woman president, remember that Muslim Pakistan has already had a woman prime minister," Mona reminded them.

"And she was assassinated, wasn't she?" retorted Elvira.

"Not for being a woman. They also kill presidents in the United States," said Mona.

He would never have the knowledge about these subjects that the present company had, thought Majnun, sipping his beer. But for this very reason he expressed his opinion in a radical manner:

"I'm going to go there."

It was the outburst of someone who couldn't resign himself to the world in which he lived. What sort of world was this where for a young person getting a job was the equivalent of winning the lottery? The best that he was able to find would be a job as uncertain as the novella he was trying to write, which had already surpassed eighty double-spaced pages, with lots of notes for the essay on tolerance in Islam. If he could, he would make reality less dense, lighter, wiping it down, simplifying it, as in the story he intended to tell. But he had a fundamental problem: he didn't know where he was, nor where to go. What sort of world was this where they killed human beings thousands of kilometers away just by pressing buttons on a computer?

In truth, he wasn't at a crossroad. At a crossroad there are possible directions and destinations. He had entered a highway with no traffic laws, where everyone was on their own, unsure of both direction and destination. He felt like one of those Americans who easily buy a machine gun to kill whoever passes in front of him. As a matter of fact, he had a revolver and, now, bullets.

"Don't be a fool, boy. You're thinking about going where, Pakistan? Or the United States?" asked his grandma Elvira.

He had received various invitations over the course of his navigations of the internet. He could join groups in Afghanistan, in Syria, in Lebanon, in Egypt, even in Ceuta and Melilla, on the African side of Spain . . . He had two problems if he were to accept: he would no longer be able to pretend that he was Muslim and Laila would never want to travel with him to such distant places.

"To Tunisia," he replied.

He wanted to go to the Middle East or North Africa. Why not Tunisia, where the government had fallen just this past January 14th? Why not witness the emergence of the revolution that everyone was discussing? Who knows, maybe even participate in it, contribute to the changes? There were other possibilities: on the 25th of that same month, protests had begun in Tahrir Square, in Cairo, calling for the resignation of President Mubarak. On the 26th, protests had also begun in Syria. And that very week when Majnun and all his grandparents were gathered on the balcony of the house, facing the pool, discussing what the newspapers called "The Arab Spring," President Mubarak had resigned on February 11th; and on the 15th, in other words, just a few days earlier, the protests against Khadafi had begun in Benghazi, Lybia.

At this moment a bee stung the arm of his grandpa Dario, who, once he felt the pain, gave his own arm a hard, but belated, slap. Elvira immediately came to his aid:

"First let's see if we can remove the stinger," she said.

Dario remained calm, with his arm extended towards his wife.

"Forget about it, my son. This is your land. If you want to be useful, there's a lot to be done right now in Brasilia," opined his grandma Mona. "And why Tunisia?"

No, there was nothing to be done in Brasilia, he thought. Here, even on social media, there was nothing but indifference. A tiny, unimportant strike here or there, but what could that lead to?

He admired his grandma Mona. He didn't only admire her. He liked her. He didn't only like her. He loved her. For that reason, he trusted her, as much as or even more than his grandpa Dario.

"Grandma," he asked her later, as they strolled through the garden together, "what if I converted to Islam?"

"That isn't something to say lightly."

"I assumed I was an atheist because I've never been to church. But, you know, I never went to church because grandpa Dario and grandma Elvira never took me. And when I started to read about Granada and the Middle East . . ."

Majnun was thinking, and a curiosity grew amidst his thoughts. Would it be indelicate to ask his grandma a question of an intimate nature? To overcome his hesitation once and for all, he abruptly inquired:

"And why don't you wear a veil?"

"Look, my son, that's not in the Koran. Not even the Bedouins wore veils."

"Is polygamy in the Koran?" he asked, thinking of Carmen and Suzana, though without renouncing his passion for Laila.

"In the *surah* about women it's said that men can marry up to four, but that, if they aren't able to be equitable with them, they should only marry one, and that this is the most suitable solution for avoiding injustices. The truth is that a man will never be equitable with more than one woman. So, the Koran is in favor of monogamy. And we live in a society in which polygamy is prohibited, even in traditionally Islamic countries. We have to be open to Allah's new creations. As it is written in the Koran, Allah is always creating."

"Well I want to get to know the Koran. Where should I start?"

"If you truly want to, start from the beginning. The first *surah*, Al-Fatiha, is the opening one. It's the one that opens the doors of paradise. It's the basis of our prayer and our faith, the one we recite in our five daily prayers. Its verses reveal the essence of Allah, his omnipresence, and also deal with the relationship between man and God."

"I'll look it up."

"They go like this:

"In the name of Allah, the Entirely Gracious, the Especially Merciful.

"All praise is due to Allah, Lord of the worlds,

"The Entirely Merciful, the Especially Merciful,

"Sovereign of the Day of Recompense.

"It is You we worship, and You we ask for help.

"Guide us to the straight path,

"The path of those upon whom You have bestowed favor, not of those who have evoked Your anger or of those who are astray."

Majnun fell pensive once more.

"There are people who don't understand," continued Mona, "but the Koran and Islam are rational. With Mohammed, humanity entered into the era of reason. In Islam, the faith itself is based on reason. Suffice it to say: the Koran demonstrates its arguments through a deductive method. What other sacred text does that? As far back as the eighth century, the *Mu'tazilis* explicated the Koran through reason and made reason the criterion for religious law. As did the philosophers. Have you ever heard of Averroes?"

"Yeah. I read a short story by Borges, in which Averroes defends the idea that the divine only knows the basic laws of the universe, the laws pertaining to the species, not to the individual."

He had also read some other quotes here and there, but he couldn't recall the sources.

"OK, well, he speaks of the harmony between religion and philosophy. When it appears that an affirmation of the Book conflicts with a philosophical proof, one must investigate it further. In the Koran, we will always find asseverations that confirm the proof."

Majnun looked up at a cloud formation. It seemed like it might rain. Then he lowered his head, wrinkled up his brows, and looked towards the house, the pool, where the blue trembled above the *azulejo* tiles, as if he were seeking some certainty about what he was hearing.

"The true Muslim knows that Allah protects him. It is not the Muslim himself, as some fanatics think, who should be protecting Allah. You should always make a distinction between Islam and

Islamism. Steer clear of the fanatics," said Mona, as if she could sense in Majnun some attraction to them.

Majnun retreated to his bedroom and surfed the internet. He read about the way that Sharia law viewed sexual desire, that *nikah* means both coitus and religious matrimony, and concluded that Islam considers sexual desire and pleasure legitimate, in this world as well as the next. They weren't sins in and of themselves, nor were they only justified in order for humanity to grow and multiply, as they were in Christianity. His grandma Mona might be right when she said that the Koran was in favor of monogamy, that it had even become the law in many Islamic countries, but his rigorous interpretation of the texts he was reading lead him to intuit that there was ample sexual liberty for men, who—as long as they respected a few rules, like being equitable and capable of supporting them—could have an unlimited number of wives, and not only because they could be married to four of them at once. They could also repudiate any of them at any time and, thus, could marry an unlimited number of times. Whereas for women, it was a whole other story, as his grandma Elvira had said.

Out of everything that Majnun read, what fascinated him most was that in various *surahs* of the Koran, some freestanding letters appeared, whose significance was uncertain to most people, and even those who claimed to know the meaning disagreed among themselves.

The theft of the dead dog

His grandpa Dario threw open his door:

"I found out that you're involved with a much older woman."

His grandpa, who had always been affable with him, had a severe expression on his face. Majnun was unsure how to respond. Why deny what his grandpa already knew?

"You're a lot older than grandma."

"It's different."

"No, it's not different at all."

"We aren't going to argue about this. I forbid you to go out with a married woman. Especially this one. Period. End this relationship now."

How had his grandpa found out? Had he been going through his computer? Reading his emails? Had he seen a photo of Laila on his Facebook page? Even she was furious that he'd been so reckless, although the name on his page was "Ibrahim" and his profile pictures weren't of him and featured different pictures every day.

His grandpa, his best friend, the same one who had told him not to miss any opportunity to have fun, was now forbidding him to see Laila!

"Are you a Muslim now? They're the ones who forbid relations outside of marriage," said Majnun.

"They're not the only ones. I'm not religious," replied his grandfather, who then shut the door as violently as he had opened it.

His grandfather had stuck his nose where it didn't belong and he lacked the moral authority to treat him that way, since, as Majnun knew, he had hardly been a saint while he lived in Paris.

Hadn't his grandpa rebelled against his own parents? Hadn't he been the only one of his siblings to leave home at odds with them all because of his politics? Hadn't he spent years being misunderstood, for being a leftist and even sympathetic to armed struggle, while his two sisters had been rock-solid anticommunists? He, Majnun, could also leave home. Besides, if he didn't want to abandon Laila, he had no other choice. He just needed to gather up his clothes, shoes, and money. So he put his best clothes into a backpack: a suit he never wore, a tie, a blue-and-white-striped linen shirt, T-shirts, and a few pairs of jeans.

He left his grandparent's house in the Dom Bosco Mansions neighborhood to hole up in a caretaker's cottage in the Parkway area. Instead of discharging his bullets into the head of Laila's husband, he discharged them—soon after arriving—in the German Shepherd who was meant to guard the country house and was showing symptoms of rabies. Then he called the veterinarian, who agreed to take care of the body.

If it weren't for the company of his laptop, his iPhone, and his iPad, his world would have been nothing more than a few square meters of cracked cement floor. The night watch and landscaping work would give him a free place to live and a little change sufficient to pay for the essential expenses: his cans of beer and his software. In his spare time—which was almost all of the time, since he didn't intend to fulfill the obligations of taking care of the country house—he'd surf the internet, brought to him by a mini-modem. He called Carmen, whom he asked if she could bring him prepared foods from her catering job once a week. Yes, she could bring a little something here and there, she replied, but he felt that trips to the market would be inevitable. He'd make do, he knew how to cook the basics. He'd avoid leaving home as much as possible.

More than what was around him, he was interested in the vast world to be discovered; the territories of absence, infinitely larger than the territory of the present, richer and more complex, a space suitable to his imagination. Perhaps for this reason he preferred strangers, whom he met on his computer. And how did these strangers behave? What did they think and say? They lived in a flexible, malleable universe, and assumed characteristics adequate to whatever their mood might be. He didn't need to feel any responsibility to them or even remember their names. Some of them didn't even have names or used pseudonyms, like him. They were like passersby spotted from afar or someone you've only heard about. He didn't need to be moved by their dramas, attenuated as they were by a hygienic distance. If he mourned their deaths or suffered with their suffering, it was because he had compassion for humanity, rather than the people as individuals. What did it matter if they wore a shirt of one color or another? That they had this name or that, this or that facial expression?

His fears were their fears. His joys were their joys, for he was aligned with them; created them in his image. In front of the computer, he therefore invented the world according to his judgment, controlled it, felt like a kid his age in front of a computer in New Mexico, launching bombs at the enemy half a world away.

A woman came through the door, and the window opened by itself, pushed ajar by a furious wind. He straightened out his shorts and quickly slipped on a black T-shirt.

"I'm Ava Gardner," she said.

It was Carmen, her lively eyes, her bright white teeth, her smile proffered, her hair, curly like his, her long, thin store-front mannequin's body, as he had seen on that first day. Just as joyful as her were her red skirt, descending halfway down her shins, yellow socks with red stripes, and a multicolored scarf draped over her white shirt.

"I imagined that only you could be such a crazy wanderer."

"I don't want to be seen by anyone," said Majnun in a somber tone.

"Who are you running from? Don't tell me it's your grandfather."

"Some time ago I dreamed a real dream that I can't forget and it explains everything: they found my legs and one of my arms floating, but the rest of my body had survived. I was here in front of my computer screen next to a woman whose eyes, now that I think of it, looked a lot like yours. There are accidents that change the future and the past, you understand? They create a new history. There are also accidents that can leave a person without legs and hands, just their head, as in the dream I had."

"What accident?" she asked, genuinely concerned.

She looked around: the bed unmade, papers strewn about the computer desk, the shoebox below the desk full of torn pieces of paper, the walls dirty, a crack in one of them, spiderwebs in the corners of the ceiling; on the desk, three thick books and, on the bed, two children's books entitled *The Legend of the Man Who Was Crazy for Laila* and *Laila and Majnun*. Carmen leafed through the two books and quickly concluded that he saw himself as Majnun, the one who was crazy for Laila. Majnun, the nickname she would give him from that point on.

"I don't know. Nothing's happened yet," he replied.

Carmen looked attentively at the cover of one of the books on the desk.

"I brought it from my grandpa's library because I'm interested in the Abencerrages."

"Abence-what?"

"The Abencerrages or Beni Seraj or even Banu Sarray or Al-Sarray, 'sons of the saddler.'"

"You and your history!"

"They were a noble lineage of Tunisian origin or else descended from an Arab tribe in Aben-Chareg, in Yemen, that accompanied the Prophet Mohammed."

"And why are you interested in that?"

"It's for my novella. I decided to set my story in the era of the fall of Granada, as famous as the fall of Troy. In Granada, in medieval Spain, some of the Abencerrages were viziers, held government positions, helped depose and reinstate rulers."

The book, explained Majnun, was a Portuguese translation from the nineteenth century of a novel by Chateaubriand, *The Adventures of the Last Abencerrage*, a Romeo-and-Juliet story in which, in the sixteenth century, a Tunisian descendant of the Abencerrages of Andalucía decided to see the land of his ancestors and fell in love with a Christian descendent of El Cid. One of the other books on the desk was the translation of a poetic fiction written by Aragon, called *Le Fou d'Elsa*. The story takes place in Granada on the eve of its fall.

"There's a verse in this book that I especially love: 'The future of man is woman. She is the color of his soul.' Despite the sad ending and a lot of things that I didn't understand, what interests me is that, as I see it, the text—which I can't tell if it's a poem or a novel—gives an apology for resistance: 'Believe in the sun when the rain is falling.' I want to see if I can also learn something or other about its technique, which mixes the past and the present. The narrator describes what the madman dreams or says like an actual crazy person, or even like someone who has dreamed about the madman."

"Enough of this madness. I came to call you back to reality. Listen here, don't you want to go outside and see some movement on the streets? That's precisely what you need to clear the nonsense from your head."

"What movement? There's no movement here," he said with displeasure, unable to imagine at that point, back in 2011, the turbulent days of 2013.

A cockroach ran across the floor of the room. He put his bare feet up on his small work desk.

"Cockroaches scare me to death," he said.

Using his flip-flop, Carmen ran after the cockroach and killed it. A viscous substance splattered on the ground. He averted his eyes and once again sat down in front of his computer screen, a window that gave out onto a world full of vanities in which he lost himself.

"The world has too many images, words, and too much information, don't you think? I want to sell silence," he said.

"Doesn't pay much. And you'd never be able to do it. You wouldn't be able to step away from that computer of yours, which, you see, has: heaps of images, words, and information. And you talk too much. For someone who lives alone, you talk too much," Carmen repeated, quickly regretting it. She didn't want to offend him.

He wrinkled his brow, his eyes fixed on a mark on the wall. It wasn't worth it to justify himself to Carmen; she had a point. He thought about saying that he talked endlessly because his mind never stopped, twirled round from one subject to the next, from one image to another.

"I dreamed of a stranger who whispered to me 'I am your destiny,'" he said.

"You dream too much. Stop dreaming and start acting."

It was a sensible order that he would only later come to understand.

"It's true. I really dreamed it. In the same dream that had a woman who looked like you. I don't believe in these sorts of things, but, if I believe in a god at all, it's the god of chance. The dream could lead me to a discovery, don't you think?" He stuck his fingers into his beard, as if he were going to comb it.

"Look, man, you're a damn good writer, you know tons of things about history, but you're gonna end up ... making yourself dumb from spending so much time with your face glued to the computer."

She thought about saying "going crazy," but he might have taken it the wrong way.

"Where did you read something I wrote?"

"I didn't. But Suzana told me that you have a lot of imagination. And you yourself told me that you're writing a story. Or aren't you?"

"I already told you, I don't want to be seen in public."

"No one is going to see you. Let's go to a little bar on the 214 North. Relax, your grandpa doesn't hang out around there. If you want to go further out, there's a nice spot close to my house in Taguatinga."

"I need to stop by the veterinarian's first."

"Let's go, then. I'll go with."

Majnun went to get the cardboard box in which he'd put the dead German Shepherd. Carmen helped him carry it to the trunk of the white Honda Civic parked at the entrance to the property.

The tires of another car squealed as someone slammed on the brakes. Three armed men got out of it. Carmen and Majnun, stupefied, didn't have time to react. A tall, muscular guy gave Majnun's frail body a shove and, with an aggressive gesture, took the car keys and the box with the dog, while the other two bandits watched him, guns in hand. In a fraction of a second, they took off with the box and the car.

"Good thing they didn't hurt us and they left my motorcycle behind," said Carmen, calmly, as if nothing had happened. "The benefits of having an old motorcycle. Do you want to go to the police station?" she asked, already moving towards the motorcycle.

"That's the only thing to do, right? I need to file a complaint."

They took off to the police station, Majnun on the back of the bike.

A chapter that, if it weren't for this warning, would leave the reader distrustful of our hero

Leaving the police station, they went to a bar on the corner of an intersection in the North Wing, at Carmen's suggestion. Majnun liked that she decided for him; that she looked after him; that she was direct, intrepid, uncomplicated, the sister he'd never had. An incestuous sister, to whom he didn't say that she was a person one could fall deeply in love with only because he was scared she would take him seriously.

Reason dictated: "Forget Laila, find some distraction, some new amusement, take off with someone else, date Carmen." But his heart was against it, that obstinate organ with a will of its own, which allowed itself to remain chained to Laila; which beat uneasily and sadly when Majnun thought of her. He would never fall in love with Carmen. And yet he wished her well. His respect for her was growing and hindered him from lying: he had to confess to her that, when it came to love, he had never experienced anything comparable to what he felt for Laila.

"Has anyone ever told you that you have the face of Lisa Gherardini?" Majnun asked.

"Who's that?"

"The wife of an old moneybag, a silk merchant named Francesco del Giocondo."

"I'm still clueless."

"Mona Lisa."

"Thanks for the praise. Man, I don't understand why you decided to turn into a recluse. Because of some bimbo ten years older than you? Forget that woman! She doesn't deserve you," said Carmen, gesticulating excitedly, shaking her head from one side to the other.

She, as always, knew everything. Had he possibly told her himself that Laila was older?

"Not ten, fifteen. Actually, you look more like Monica Bellucci," he said, lowering his voice as if he were revealing a secret.

"Stop it," she replied, with a smile of satisfaction.

"Has any man ever fallen in love with you?" he asked, looking down at their glasses of beer.

"Are you trying to offend me?"

"Why would that offend you? No one has ever fallen in love with me. The person who I thought loved me no longer does."

"She doesn't deserve you."

"But what about you? Has any man ever fallen in love with you?"

"And why would it have to be a man?"

"As far as I know, you're not a lesbian."

"But even so, some woman could have fallen in love with me."

"Well, did that ever happen?"

Was he insinuating that no one was capable of falling in love with her?

"A guy was in love with me for two years," she replied, somewhere between jesting and serious.

"And you didn't love him back?"

"I didn't even know the dude," she said, laughing.

"How is that?"

"He fell in love with a picture of me on Facebook. A nut just like you, glued to the net. The guy was from Cuiabá, and I was living in Crato. He sent me messages, wanted to meet me. And I'd respond politely. And three years passed like that, can you believe it! With him proposing to come see me; me saying that it was best if he didn't. Until one day I got a phone call. I'm in Fortaleza, he said, I came to see you. I don't know how he tracked down my phone number. I don't have much time today, I replied, just two free hours in the afternoon. And it was true, since I also worked nights. Yet he still came, traveled the seven hours from Fortaleza to Crato to see me for two hours. And the story ended there, after three years. We never corresponded again."

"And why are you telling me this silly story?"

"Well, because you asked. And also to say that sometimes, when you meet someone in person, the charm disappears. So perhaps you're right to stay holed up with your computer. Man, this stuff with your grandfather is bullshit. He must be worried. Is your grandpa's nickname Náfita?"

"From naphthalene—the mothball stuff—or some character from a novel, it's Naphta with a 'ph,' some cruel joke of grandma Elvira's. She, in turn, got the nickname Settembrina, I think because she was born on September 17th."

"From what you've told me, this grandfather of yours sounds wonderful."

"He was. I know he's been going nuts over me leaving home. But I called, told them I was well, that I'm not going to run wild, that I won't waste money willy-nilly, and that there's no point in calling the police. I made up a story that I was going to travel throughout the Northeast."

He didn't tell Carmen that his grandpa was furious that he'd withdrawn everything from their joint savings account at the bank, the first time he'd ever touched the money in that account, into which his grandpa had been making deposits ever since Majnun was a child. His grandpa had told him that that money would come in handy for him one day in the future. For Majnun, that day had arrived. He needed cash in hand, because he didn't want to use his credit card, so he wouldn't leave clues as to where he was.

"I don't want anything to do with Grandpa Dario any more. And I never liked Grandma Elvira. I'm sick of living with them. They argue about everything, even novels, like *Quincas Borba*. Grandma quoted this passage about the 'party of convenience,' which yields to power and supports corrupt, worthless people. She only concerns herself with day-to-day practical things: what brand of TV to buy, if she should give change to the beggar on the corner, if she should fire the maid from Pernambuco who has lived with us forever . . . At most, she hopes to improve the quality of public services, while Dario, on the other hand, wants to solve the world's problems. He says that piety and charity are pointless if they don't change society. Grandma thinks that this is callousness in the face of the suffering of others. For him, anything revolutionary is good, and it's necessary to leap over the rotten side of history. So Grandma asks him: do you think that time lets you leap for free? It'll avenge those leaps later, charging interest on the parts that were leapt over, time doesn't pass or leap, we're the ones who pass through it, accumulating surprises and wrinkles. Even the young grow old, she always says."

"And which of them is right?"

"I would like to fight for grand causes, I just don't know which ones."

"Stop wanting to be the navel of the world."

"Did you know that Hemingway, John Dos Passos, and Dorothy Parker were all in Spain during the civil war there? And that André Malraux, George Orwell, and Simone Weil all took up arms? But today . . . what cause is there for me to fight for? All the novelty is in the Middle East, in the Arab countries. All it took was for some unknown guy named Mohamed Bouazizi to set himself on fire. It was the spark in the powder keg. It blew up everything. I wish I was in the center of all those events, in Tunis . . . Or else join up with the angry crowds in Spain."

"You can just join one of the gangs around here, become a skin-head, buy some chains . . ."

"No, that's racist, far-right stuff . . . I'm not interested in gangs."

"Suzana is going to Spain."

Suzanas thighs, her legs crossing and uncrossing, immediately occupied Majnun's mind. Would they get in the way of his conversion to Islam? No, Islam valued the rights of the body, as he'd read.

"Sometimes I get this impression that I lived in Spain during the Middle Ages, that I lived in the Alhambra. The novella that I'm writing is about that. Because of my grandma Mona, who lives in São Paulo, sometimes I feel like I'm half Arabic. And because of my grandpa Sérgio, half Spanish."

He quickly adjusted his tone of voice, which would have led one to believe he had put a period at the end of that sentence, as if he wanted swiftly to correct what he'd said:

"But my dark skin and curly hair are certainly of African origin, which has nothing to do with my parents or my grandparents. And I feel like I'm Americanized from the movies I watch and the music

I listen to. Deep down, I don't belong to any place at all."

"Tell me the plot of your short story. Or is it a novella?"

She didn't have to beg, since for a long time he had wanted someone to listen to the story and offer critique:

"It's like this: as you know, the Catholic monarchs Fernando and Isabella made decrees that proclaimed the purity of the blood and the orthodoxy of the faith in order to drive not only the Muslims, but also the Jews, out of the Iberian Peninsula. So, for my novella I created a Jewish character. He's an interpreter. The last sultan of Granada, Boabdil, had two Jewish interpreters: Isaac Perdoniel and his son-in-law Yehuda. Well then, my character is the third interpreter of the Sultan. I'm going to name him Aarón. His wife will be named Sulamita. And I invented three children for this couple. Aarón speaks perfect Ladino, the Spanish from the fifteenth century that contains Arabic, Balkan, French, and Portuguese words. He's friends with the last Jewish poet of Sefarad — Sefarad is the Hebrew name for Spain. This poet is the scholar of Granada Se'adiyah Ibn Danan who, in the tradition of Maimonides, composed his written works in Arabic. What I've got to decide is whether the novella is going to end in tragedy because of the Christian occupation or, thanks to the intercession of a character named Ibrahim, have a hopeful ending. Ibrahim is the first-person narrator. If it were to be a tragedy, Aarón would be among the 120,000 to 150,000 Jews expulsed by the 1492 Alhambra decree. The Inquisition, which, in the hands of the Pope and bishops, wasn't very powerful, was transforming into the terrible tribunal in the hands of the Spanish monarchs. Aarón didn't have anywhere to escape to, since the Jews had already been expulsed from the rest of Europe. Like many others, he decided to take his family to Portugal, but the Inquisition Tribunal soon arrived there too. As such, the novella is going to end in Fez, Morocco, the place where his friend, the last poet of Granada, took refuge and died in December of 1492. Fez was also where Boabdil found himself after the capitulation and an interregnum in the fiefdom of the Alpujarras. I'm going to infuse an admiration for Boabdil into my Jewish character. Not just admiration. Love. That way the novella will also dialogue with those who mistakenly see something feminine in Boabdil as a result of a legend invented by the Christians, according to which his mother said to him, after the capitulation, on the hill that became known as 'The Moor's Sigh': 'don't cry like a woman over that which you couldn't defend like a man.' At the end of the novella, when Boabdil is merely a prince taken in by the sultan in Fez, Aarón takes part in a battle with Boabdil, in 1533, and dies at his side in a Romeo-and-Juliet story, in which Boabdil never suspects the platonic love of his friend."

Majnun sought approval in Carmen's face. He saw only astonishment.

"I really wanted to get to know Spain, become reacquainted with my ancestors," he added.

"Why don't you go? If you go, I will too."

"It's difficult."

"You deserve some fun. Suzana is going to Catholic World Youth Day. She's staying for a month."

He could still see, as if it weren't all in his imagination, Suzana's thighs.

"I'm not Catholic," he said, almost adding "and I want to convert to Islam."

"Suzana is half Jewish."

"And she's going to a Catholic gathering?"

Suzana was so full of herself. But how could he forget that body he'd studied that day by the pool at the club?

"Only her dad is Jewish."

"And you? Are you Catholic?"

Her time in the Catholic Church had produced in Carmen affection for Evangelicals, who sang upbeat songs, supported each other, and were practical. For them, the kingdom of heaven was closer to Earth than it was in Catholicism with its stories of the lives of the saints. But lately she identified as a Spiritist.

"Why do you ask? Do I have to be Catholic to go to Spain?"

"You said that Suzana's going to a Catholic gathering."

"We don't have to go with her."

"Well then, how about it? Are you Catholic?"

"I go to the Garden of Salvation."

"Will you take me there?"

"Why?"

"Curiosity."

"If it's only out of curiosity, forget it."

"I'm in the middle of a spiritual journey. I want to believe in something, follow a religion. Because my grandparents raised me this way, without a religion. Do you believe in reincarnation?"

"I do. Why do you ask?"

"In a previous incarnation I lived in Granada, during the time of Sultan Boabdil."

The clear sky, a bluish color, recalled the Magritte painting *L'Empire des lumières*, in which the light of day, still visible in the sky of the canvas, contrasts with the light of night that is seen below: a glowing streetlamp, the illuminated windows of a house. A strange, banal painting. The stolen car was nothing. Majnun expected miracles, foresaw disasters.

Which dead person to contact?

Two days after their trip to the police station, on a hot, sunny Sunday, as they arrived at the Garden of Salvation, Carmen and Majnun sat down on a dark-blue bench. He had a bottle of water, out of which he was constantly drinking. An old man with light-colored eyes and white hair and beard, resting on a gold bench, got up and walked over to him:

"Can I sit down beside you?"

Majnun, silent, offered no opposition. Carmen, seemingly annoyed, walked over towards the lake.

"I understand your anguish and suffering," said the old man in a French accent. "You, like everyone else, are looking for the answer to two questions: Who am I? And why am I here? I'll give you the answers: you aren't a reflection; the reflection is you. Change your gaze and the world changes. Every element that is here can be arranged in a different way, seen in another manner. The world consists of suffering. And the illusion is what creates this suffering. Free yourself of your illusions and cast a free glance upon the world."

"Are you French, Sir?"

"Belgian."

He put a hand on Majnun's shoulder and continued, his voice hoarse:

"I was watching. I heard your friend say that you've abandoned everything. Know that the young prince Buddha did that too. He even abandoned his child and wife. He traded a sheltered, worry-free life for contact with suffering, ugliness, and death. Suffering is the culmination of human life, the inseparable companion of perception. There's no use in trying to take refuge in sensual or mental pleasure, for they lead to even greater pain. The only refuge is knowledge. Look at these cards. On each one there are teachings taken from the Mahabharata. In a moment of doubt, you shuffle the cards and choose one. You'll see how many teachings there are. Try it out. Take one."

Majnun felt hypnotized, less by the hoarse words than by the hot sun. He pulled a card out of what seemed to him a deck of playing cards and read: "Action is preferable to renunciation."

"What do you think it means?"

Was it what Carmen had wanted to tell him? Majnun thought about replying to the old man that action only made sense if there was a future and that he didn't believe in the future. That the future, contrary to the present, was, by definition, distant. That action only made sense if there was a result now, in the present, this present that was intermixed with what he, Majnun, was. That he didn't want to disguise his present, especially not in a disguise of future and hope. The good thing about the present was that it promised nothing. It just was. But this thought, though clear, didn't come to him in words that were easy to articulate, but with snippets of silence.

The old man seemed to guess at it when he refuted him:

"You only live and understand the present because you believe in the future. Look at my story: I came to Brazil in the seventies. I decided to isolate myself on a beach in the Northeast and live there for the rest of my life. Later, I kept on traveling. I lived in India and Nepal, where I have a guru. Then I came here and, instead of staying holed up and waiting for someone to come looking for me, I look around me and find those that need me. I try to help because I believe in the future."

Majnun rifled through his bag for a notebook in order to jot down an idea that he'd later toss into his shoebox: reconcile the times, the immediate, what will happen tomorrow, and what will manifest itself decades from now or even after death. He couldn't find his notebook; he'd forgotten to bring it. The idea would be lost.

After a pause, the old man said:

"Think in an objective manner. What does the teaching on this card mean to you?"

Majnun looked at it again: "Action is preferable to renunciation." He thought: instead of voyaging around the internet and taking Laila on imaginary travels, he should really travel, convince Laila to steal away with him, far away, to Spain. If she was really just afraid of her husband, they'd be safe. His heart palpitated with the thought of

Laila, of that trip.

"I don't know," he answered.

"Take another."

He mechanically pulled one out and read: "Being captive to something we don't love means suffering. Being separated from what we do love means suffering. Not having what we desire means suffering. Suffering is a lack of love. Those who deserve life deserve love, and vice versa. Living to love and loving to live."

"Live a lot to suffer a lot?" he thought.

"Love has no commerce, nor gain, nor fear," said the old man. "I'm selling these cards really cheap. Take them, my son. They'll do you good. Want one?" The old man handed him a joint.

"I don't take hallucinogens."

"I would call it a 'lucinogen,'" replied the old man. And continued: "The Mahabharata is a grand book of wisdom, especially one of its parts, the Bhagavad Gita. I took much of what I've learned from it. For example, that a man cannot free himself from action by not carrying out his work, nor achieve happiness by abstaining from all action. No one can remain inactive for a single instant. You're wrong to close yourself off, not want to see anybody, as your friend said. Action is superior to inaction. The result doesn't matter, as long as we do what we must."

"I don't have the energy for that."

"What is energy? It's the courage to do what's right. And what are the enemies of energy? Indolence, love of evil, dejection, and self-hatred."

The cards seemed, to Majnun, to contain wisdom. The first commanded him to travel; the second, to live for loving Laila.

When Carmen returned, Majnun bought the deck from the old man and followed her to the lake's edge, water bottle in hand, now almost empty.

"The sun is going to start to set, and I want you to participate in a Spiritist session."

"Will they allow me in?"

"The medium is my friend."

While Carmen made the contacts necessary to secure his presence, Majnun sat down at the edge of the lake and examined the deck of cards. A bell rang. By chance, his eyes rested upon a card that confused him: "He whose action is guided by desire is imprisoned by desire. Liberate yourself from desire." Abandon Laila? Never. Those cards weren't infallible. He started typing an email to Laila on his iPhone, still unsure of what to say. Or perhaps the desire he should free himself from was his desire for Suzana?

Carmen interrupted him and took him to a windowless room. Majnun looked around: a solitary candle shining in the middle of an oval table; a slender believer, her face pallid and frightened, seated at the table covered in white cloth; the instructor—a short woman with chubby arms—was standing; incense burning on a small side table. Water bottle still in hand, Majnun waited for them to show him where to go. The instructor asked him to come over to the oval table.

"We are going to perform this session with the minimum number of believers allowed, which is to say: three."

It would only be him, Carmen, and the slender young woman.

The medium was also seated at the table, across from the slender young woman, a Spiritist book in front of her and a jar of water to her right. Her face, on which was drawn a straight-lined mouth with almost no lips, matched her faded blue dress, as inelegant as a nun's.

A Bach sonata floated from two speakers in the corners of the room.

The instructor asked if anyone was carrying glass or minerals, which might interfere with the reception of the spirits. No one was.

"Any cell phones? They should be turned off, not just silenced. Electronic devices could create an interference."

Majnun switched off his iPhone.

"People, positive attitudes! Without it the session might not go right," said the instructor, looking at the incredulous Majnun.

She turned on the recorder and opened the session with a prayer, requesting the protection of the spirits of light. She grabbed a Bible and read Psalm 23:

God is my shepherd; I shall not want.

He maketh me to lie down in green pastures; he leadeth me beside the still waters.

He restoreth my soul; he leadeth me in the paths of righteousness for his own name's sake.

Yea, though I walk through the valley of the shadow of death, I will fear no evil: for thou art with me; thy rod and thy staff they comfort me.

Thou preparest a table before me in the presence of mine enemies; thou anointest my head with oil; my cup runneth over.

Surely goodness and mercy shall follow me all the days of my life; and I will dwell in the house of the Lord forever.

She then asked the three of them to put their hands, palms up, on the table.

The medium intervened:

"Each one of you should concentrate on the deceased person you wish to contact."

Carmen put a photograph of her half-brother — from her mom's side — on the table. Majnun tried to put out of his mind the twelve knife blows and copious blood from the story that Carmen had told him.

"Are you there? Can you answer me?" Carmen asked.

The spirit of her brother didn't take long to make himself present. Guided by Carmen's questions, he confirmed the afflicted state of his soul and asked for prayers to free him from it.

When Carmen's predictable conversation with her brother — who might have still been floating around the room — came to an end, there was an even more frightened expression on the slender young woman's face. Her eyes, fixed on the darkness in the back of the room, seemed to spy some spirit coming through the wall.

Majnun had a fixed idea: contact Boabdil. He imagined him with a grayish beard, premature wrinkles for a thirty year-old man, his eyelids fallen, and his red turban just the way he'd seen it in an image on the internet.

"I see that a spirit has responded to your call," said the medium, looking at Majnun. "Ask if it's the spirit you were thinking about."

/ 68

"Are you the spirit I was thinking about?" Majnun inquired, repeating the medium's words like an automaton.

"Yes," replied the medium.

"Boabdil?"

"Yes," confirmed the medium.

"What do you want from me?"

"That sort of question doesn't work," said Carmen, clarifying. "It has to be a yes or no question."

"Do you want me to save the Alhambra from the Catholic invasion?"

"Yes."

"Is it still possible?"

"Yes."

"Should I travel to Granada to do so?"

"Yes."

Apparently the spirit only knew how to say "yes," he thought.

"Can I play a part similar to that of Ibrahim?"

"Yes."

"And could I also prevent the war fought by you, Sir, against your father and your uncle?"

"No."

"Should I ally myself with the Abencerrages?"

"Yes."

Majnun had read many different versions of the story of the Abencerrages, in addition to hearing Professor Rodrigo's version. The most probable story was that many of them had been decapitated in the room of the Alhambra that is today known as the Hall of the Abencerrages, and that Boabdil's father, under advice from the Vizier Abul Cacim Venegas, had ordered the massacre. He had also read in Washington Irving the legend that the blood of the victims could still be seen in the fountain of that same room and that, underneath the nearby Court of the Lions, the sounds of chains made by their troubled spirits could be heard.

Majnun knew of the Abencerrages principally through the accounts of the war between Boabdil and his father. After the conversation with Professor Rodrigo Díaz, he had read that, with the help of his mother—Fátima or Aixa—and that of the Abencerrages, Boabdil took control of his father's throne in 1482. The father, to defend himself against his son, fled Granada with his brother, Mohammed XIII, Abu Abd Allah Mohammed, also called "el Zagal" (which meant "the valiant"). In 1485, Boabdil's father was on his deathbed and named his brother as his successor. From that point on, the war was between uncle and nephew.

When her turn arrived, the slender young woman burst into a convulsive crying fit.

"No, I don't want to," she sobbed.

"You are very sensitive, my daughter. Calm down. Ask if this is the spirit you were thinking about."

The young woman was crying louder and louder. The instructor went up behind her and put her hands on the young woman's shoulders, as if she were giving her a massage.

"No, I don't want to speak to her," the young woman finally said, resolute and angry.

"You're not ready, my daughter. Let's try again when you have calmed down," said the medium.

An hour had passed, and the instructor read a prayer of gratitude to the spirits and closed the session with the following words:

"Return in peace to the world of the spirits."

"The circle may now be broken," said the medium.

There wasn't any circle at all. Majnun understood that it meant he could take his hands off the table.

The medium asked them to prepare themselves for a blessing. That they concentrate. That they summon the desire to receive it. Without that desire, the blessing wouldn't work.

"It will do you much good," she said to the slender young woman, who had stopped sobbing.

Majnun looked inquisitively at Carmen.

"It's a magnetic transmission of energetic fluids," she explained. "From perispirit to perispirit."

"Perispirit?"

"You're in need of it," she said. "You have problems of obsessive origin."

"Me?"

Carmen couldn't clarify further. She merely hoped that Majnun would be freed of his obsession for Laila.

Majnun assumed the posture of a patient in order to receive the medium's blessings.

She began to give the individual, isolated blessings, starting with the slender young woman. When Majnun's turn arrived, she said:

"You're in luck, this blessing won't merely pertain to the soul."

Majnun again looked inquisitively, this time at the medium.

"What I mean to say is that the spirit has decided to return."

"Who, Boabdil?"

"Yes, the same spirit that was here before. Thus I can give you a mediumistic blessing. The spirit will act upon you fluidly and mag-netically."

She stood, raising her hands above Majnun, who was seated. Then she slowly passed her hands down the length of his body, without touching it.

Five minutes later the blessing had been given and received.

"You can drink water from the jar, which was transformed by the spirit during the vibration," she said to Majnun.

"No, I prefer not to," he replied, doubting that the spirit had killed all the bacteria in that dirty water.

"Then you can put some in your bottle and take it home," she suggested.

Carmen took the bottle from his hand and filled it to the top.

They were walking back to the entrance to the Garden of Salva-tion when the night began to invade the landscape, yellowed by the dryness of the season. The dirt path passed the back of a squat building: a kitchen, judging by the smell and the enormous trash-cans. Then it curved and rose, bordered by stones and bushes with dried-out flowers. Other people followed close by, laughing and talk-ing loudly.

"Do you think there's some Spanish person here feeding information to the medium?" Majnun asked.

"It isn't a trick. The spirits really come down here. I've witnessed a lot of sessions. And you have mediumistic powers. I could feel how quickly you attracted the spirit, how he was at your disposal . . ."

"Is it always famous people?"

"A deceased relative, a father, a mother, a daughter. Didn't you notice that I summoned my brother? Have you been there before? I mean, to Granada?" asked Carmen.

"I've never even been to Spain. It wouldn't be a bad idea to join up with Suzana on this trip."

They walked slowly, listening to the sounds of their shoes, since the people who were following them had already passed. Carmen finally asked:

"Can I come with you?"

"If you don't mind going with me and Laila . . ."

"That isn't over yet?"

Without replying, he dialed Laila's number. She didn't pick up.

He sent a text:

"comin ovr"

"don't even think abt it," she immediately replied.

"be there in half an hour"

"don't come! very dangerous"

"want to run off with me to Spain?"

"ur crazy!"

Before I finally go insane

The following morning, Majnun sat down in front of his computer before eating breakfast. Oh, that he might reignite a fervent passion in Laila! He would lead her through the whole complex geography of his feelings. That he could once again submerge himself in that tall, plump body, in her large breasts. He didn't just want to meet up with her one afternoon in a motel, but in some eternal place, hidden from the world, where they could stroll tranquilly under moon and sun, holding back neither tears nor laughter. He wanted to embrace her inside a white house with vaulted ceilings, with room enough for dreams, imagination, and mellow music, like that first night. Music that would hold them in an abiding dance, with no distinction between present and future. What more did they need? With very little they could build a new world. Suddenly he feared that his love for Laila was like that of Qays for Layla in the Eastern legend, love at first sight, love that would remain forbidden until the death of both lovers, who would never see each other again.

He searched YouTube for the Eric Clapton song. He listened to it three times in a row:

> *Layla, you've got me on my knees.*
> *Layla, I'm begging, darling please.*
> *Layla, darling won't you ease my worried mind.*
>
> *I tried to give you consolation.*
> *When your old man had let you down.*
> *Like a fool, I fell in love with you,*
> *Turned my whole world upside down.*
> *(. . .)*
> *Let's make the best of the situation*
> *Before I finally go insane.*
> *Please don't say I'll never find a way*
> *And tell me all my love's in vain.*

He asked himself what name and face he should have that day. The sun was setting the horizon aflame on the other side of the window. Like a spotlight upon a stage, it illuminated the landscape between the shadows of scant clouds. In front of the computer, he was both nowhere and many places at once. He was the hero, the dashing adventurer, the famous and beloved celebrity, whom nobody knew personally. He had already been Humphrey Bogart, James Dean, Marlon Brando, and Elvis Presley. What face would he have that day? He needed to choose another photograph for his profile.

Was that what it meant to be a person in this day and age? He had a feeling that it was not; that he lived outside of his own time on fiber-optic cables and in the fidgety minds of virtual friends. His roots spread throughout the world, extending out from place to place. They weren't even roots, too shallow for that. He glided through the air, from one season to the next, carried along flying rivers.

Who was he, truly? Would he find out some day? He searched his own name on Google. "It's here, I exist." He read the autobiographical note he'd sent in to the short story contest: "When I was a child, I wanted to be an aviator. I've always enjoyed studying history . . ." Ah, his face that day could be that of Ezra Pound in a photo taken by Cartier-Bresson in 1971, which he had just stumbled upon. There it was. But was that really Ezra Pound's face? He always mixed up people's faces.

If he chose the right profile picture, a playful, bodyless God would knock on his door, and he would be filled with enthusiasm.

No, no God would come, but rather the devil. Indeed, because, unlike the heaven of the gods—purely fictional—hell really existed and wasn't a supernatural reality. It existed on Earth, in that city, in that desert, in that era of want, of absence, in which he felt abandoned by Laila, in that moment in which a gust of hot wind descended like jet exhaust on him, spraying dust particles onto his face, messing up his hair. Hell wasn't where he was headed, it was where he'd fled from and where he lived. It wasn't inhabited by sinners, but by innocents like him.

"I already know, I'm going to have the face of pain," he thought, remembering that, in the dream in which he was nothing more than a head, a child had given him a book. He remembered it now; it had a red cover with gold inscriptions: *El libro de Dolores*. He typed "El libro de Dolores" in Google. That was it, it had to do with pain: pain of the soul and of the body. The greatest pain was when the heart throbbed with love.

Naturally, the search results pertained to "libro" and, thus, were all in Spanish. Majnun found a preface to a book that talked about the irreparable pain of the loss of a loved one, as well as a text about the two-month captivity of a São Paulo businessman who had been kidnapped.

In the third search result—an essay on Aristotle, whom Averroes had introduced to the Europeans—the words "*dolores*" and "*libro*" appeared separately and far from each other. The text on the ontological priority of substance, understood as a place and subject of change, asserted that language was only possible if words had meaning. Otherwise, it was noise. "I speak noise," he wrote down on a scrap of paper, which he then tossed into the shoebox. The Aristotle of Google referred to things he was thoroughly interested in: History, which relates what has happened, unlike Poetry, which delved into what may happen.

Another attempt on Google: *El libro de Dolores* didn't exist. The search yielded a review of two other books, *The Man Who Believed He Was Wagner* and *The Diary of Inés*, complimentary novels published by an Argentine publishing house. The man who believed he was Wagner was a young romantic, like him, though he had an athletic body, in contrast to Majnun's. The Inés of the diary, for her part, was beautiful and a recent arrival from Madrid. She had Suzana's face and body. Each author had written a diary about the love between them. Stories of adolescents filled with of drugs, sex, passionate political debates, and quotes from songs and films. The poorly written review, in which the word "*dolores*" appeared a single time, considered the end of the story, where the two novels intertwined, to be quite surprising.

"Inés is dead," said Majnun aloud, determined to abandon his attempt at finding a photo for that day's profile. And then he remembered Ibrahim. Ibrahim, of course! Ibrahim! He couldn't find a convincing photo of Ibrahim, unless Ibrahim was the astrologer in a three-act opera by Nikolai Rimsky-Korsakov, inspired by a poem by Pushkin and entitled "The Golden Cockerel." Could be, why not? There was a photograph of the astrologer who protected the kingdom of King Dodon from invasion, using as his weapon a golden cock that crows at times of danger. Majnun envisioned himself dressed in the same white astrakhan fur hat and the same blue tunic spotted with golden stars, ready to defend not Dodon, but Granada.

In which ingenious Majnun, the adventurer, leaves his homeland for the first time

He went onto the World Youth Day site, researched the different types of registration, and called Carmen.

"What do you think? Should we register as individuals or as a group?"

"What are you talking about?"

"The World Youth Day, in Madrid."

"That's nuts! When did you become a Catholic?"

"It's a chance to go to Spain, like you said."

"Yeah, but I don't want to go under the patronage of the Pope. I sent an email to Pablo, the son of the Spanish professor we met. I asked if he could write the invitation letter necessary for entry into the country."

"Let's buy a package without a meal plan. It costs 133 euros a week. I have to put in the info for the responsible party, which is to say: me."

"Just the two of us isn't a group."

"And by yourself you're not going to get into Spain."

"I'm not going to lie and I don't want to waste my time trying to see the Pope."

"I'm going to register as an individual then."

He looked over the site once more. She was right, there was no use in lying unless it was something essential. He had to put in all of his information: first name, last name, date and city of birth, e-mail address (he was going to create a new one just for this), address, telephone number, and national ID number. So stupid! On the internet for two minutes and he already had to reveal his identity in full detail, shit! Even though he didn't have any true identity? Even though he didn't know who he really was?

He called Suzana. She was a spoiled brat, so why would she want to venture out on the trip like that with thousands of other young people? Indeed, a spoiled brat, nice to those she wanted to be nice to; rude to the rest of humanity. But he had to admit that it would be awesome to travel with her just to admire the shapes of her body, poorly hidden by her tight dresses, shapes that he'd had the good fortune to examine with his naked eye at the Cota Mil pool. She was a taller, lighter-skinned Laila, with long, flowing, fair hair.

"Would it be possible for me to join your group?" he asked.

"In that case you'd have to choose the same parish."

"That's fine. I want to room with a big group, not end up in staying with some host family."

"Well I don't want to stay in a school or a convent or a gym, much less in the house of some host family. I'm staying in a hotel. I can't decide between one in Malasaña, one in Chueca, and another on the Calle de Alcalá, close to the Puerta del Sol."

"It's cheaper to stay at a school or a gym," maintained Majnun.

"I prefer my comforts."

On that same day Majnun received the insurance money from his car and he felt rich. The money from the savings plus the insurance money would allow him not to worry about being frugal on the trip and this was a motivation to insist with Laila again. If she accepted, he would take off with her, preferably to the Northeast. And if she didn't accept, who knows, maybe Suzana would share a room with him in Madrid? He would trade happiness — that obscure, abstract feeling — for pleasure — clear and concrete.

He had a premonition that something terrible was going to occur. He urgently needed to see Laila. He put the revolver in his pocket. But unless it was absolutely necessary, he wasn't going to shoot that repulsive husband.

An hour and a half later, he got off the bus and walked down a deserted street to the lakefront property in Lago Norte where Laila lived. He hesitated and made an about-face when he got to the two cars parked in front of the house. He mustered the courage with difficulty, filled his lungs with air, and rang the doorbell. A servant told him that Laila didn't want to see him. But her husband did.

"You aren't welcome here," said, irritably, the tall guy in a brown suit. He had big ears, a gold earring in one of them, and a long chin covered by a thick, unkempt beard.

Majnun stared at him with his best tough-guy expression.

"I'm warning you," said Laila's husband, raising his voice. "Get out of here, you bastard. What do you want with Laila? She doesn't even want to hear about you. Look here, you son of a bitch, she doesn't want to see you. And if you ever show up here again, I'll finish you."

Majnun turned around, defeated. But out of this feeling of defeat, rebellion emerged. Now or never, he would confront that detestable guy.

"You're the son of a bitch. I'm going to kill you," said Majnun, with a hand in his pocket, on the revolver.

When Laila's husband made a move to attack him, he pulled the revolver out of his pocket in a gesture that fell short of being courageous only because he did it without a thought.

Laila's husband wasn't intimidated. He moved towards him and grabbed his arm. Majnun then fired a shot towards the roof of the garage. He managed to break free from the grasp of that repulsive guy and ran off in a hurry—defeated and on the lam—down the street, which remained deserted.

Along the way, he recalled a *surah* in the Koran which, according to some, could be invoked to ward off the evil eye. On a bus heading towards the Pilot Plan area of Brasilia, sitting beside a woman with a yellowish face marked with suffering, a serious expression, and a plucked mustache above her meaty lips, he did a quick search on his iPhone and finally read aloud:

114th Sura
The Mankind
Revealed in Mecca.
In the name of God, the Most Gracious, the Most Merciful.
Say: "I seek refuge in the Lord of mankind,
The Sovereign of mankind,
The God of mankind,
From the evil of the retreating whisperer,
Who whispers into the breasts of mankind,
From among the jinn and mankind."

He felt protected. The woman beside him looked at him as if he were crazy, and only then did he notice that her eyes were her saving grace: deep, inquisitive eyes, large and beautiful.

Once home, he received an email from an unknown address: "change your email address." He knew it was Laila. If she were telling him to change his email address, then it wasn't true that she didn't want to see him. He created a new email and sent her a single query: "Is it you?"

"Flee," she replied, "don't go out in public, he's going to report you to the police."

On the night before his departure to Madrid, Majnun had a dream. In the darkness of night, he spotted Laila's house. It was difficult to distinguish outlines in that darkened landscape. Anguished, he fired bullets from the revolver at Laila's husband as he was getting out of a red car. The bullets hit his grandpa Dario, seated at his desk, which only now could Majnun see back behind the garage. The blood ran onto the ground below, then climbed one of the walls. It started to drip from the roof, drop by drop, unhurriedly, soaking the pillow and the mattress. Majnun awoke with no idea where he was, perhaps a side effect of his sleeping pill. His body was trembling. He examined the revolver which was underneath his pillow. All the bullets had been fired. When? Where?

He hid the revolver. He dug a hole beneath a cashew tree on the property of the country estate, a beautiful cashew tree that produced large, red cashew fruits with juice as red as the juice from the famous and world's largest cashew tree in the city of Natal.

He didn't tell his grandparents about the trip, which would last as long as his money would allow. He didn't want to leave a trail at banks or by using credit cards. His faithful companions — iPhone, iPad, and laptop — were in his backpack.

At Guarulhos Airport, where they had a layover, Majnun, Carmen, and Suzana were waiting for the flight to Madrid, he and Carmen in jeans and the yellow jersey of the Brazilian national soccer team. Majnun had bought a package from the World Youth Day, but decided against staying with a host family or at a gym when Suzana accepted the idea of the three of them sharing a room.

"I hate terrorists. They took all the pleasure out of travel. Because of them you can't even pack a suitcase properly," said Suzana, taking the headphones from her iPod out of her ears.

"I'm going to disappear. You two should forget about me," said Majnun, agitated, as if he hadn't heard Suzana.

How he missed Laila! He had to admit it, he was traveling in order to forget her. Ah, Laila, why had she abandoned him? Cruel Laila, who allowed her heart to be dominated by fear.

"Don't say such silly things, not even as a joke," said Carmen.

"I feel an ominous premonition about this. I shouldn't take this trip. I don't think it's going to be good for any of us. And that's putting it lightly. It's going to be a tragedy. There's still time to turn back," said Majnun.

"Dude, what's up with you? You're complicated, huh?" replied Carmen.

"Will you two take care of me?"

"Don't count on me," responded Suzana, putting the headphones of her iPod back in her ears.

"You won't need us to," asserted Carmen.

On the plane, Majnun read the email, from Laila's new address, that had just appeared on his iPhone:

"just want to know if it really was you. where r u?"

"if what was me?" he replied.

"u know."

He didn't know. The flight was about to take off, and cell phones had to be switched off.

Montaigne, Diogenes, and a sink

With the tropics behind them, thought Majnun, there was less of everything: fewer birds, fewer palm trees, less green, less water, less noise, less emotion ... Even fear was diminished, while the plane rose, rose, and rose even more still. It flew free and high. The fasten-seatbelts sign was turned off, and the pilot told them that electronic devices could be turned back on in airplane mode.

Majnun looked at Suzana's long thighs, crossed underneath her black skirt and covered by dark but transparent silk tights, which she would certainly have to remove when the Madrid heat hit them. He was aroused as he leaned his thigh against Suzana's. He pretended to be asleep and gently let his head come to rest on her shoulder.

A few minutes later, she moved her shoulder away from him.

He went to the bathroom to do in private that which Montaigne claimed Diogenes did in public in order to satisfy his lust. He looked down at his cock, feeling the erection between his fingers. Joy blossomed from deep in his guts, together with a feeling of suffering at not being able to hold Suzana tight and ejaculate on her. He lined the sink with paper towels, held his cock over the paper, and began to masturbate, seeing, as if he were watching a movie, Suzana's vulva and enormous ass. He imagined entering Suzana with agile movements, moving back and forth above the sink. He came harder than he had in a very long time. He looked down at the amount of semen he'd ejaculated, which was running down the sink. More than usual.

When he returned to his seat, Suzana was sleeping with a red blanket covering her whole body. Majnun thought about finding one of her hands underneath the blanket and holding hands with her for the rest of the plane ride. Then he fell asleep.

He dreamed of Carmen, Suzana, and Laila, all three graces in the same dream, in a courtyard where *macumba* is practiced, each of them playing a marimba, wearing only bikini bottoms, their breasts bouncing. Laila's husband was spraying bullets with a machine gun every which way. He, Majnun, was able to defend against it with difficulty, jumping from one place to the next. Suddenly, for some inexplicable reason—or perhaps because he thought they were the guilty ones—he pointed his revolver at the three women. They screamed, kneeled before him, begged forgiveness. Forgiveness for what? he asked himself, indignant. From one moment to the next, Laila turned into Moraima, the wife of Sultan Boabdil, extremely beautiful in an outfit made of turquoise-colored cloth with golden threads, and Carmen was Moraima's slave. Carmen, covered in emerald necklaces and seated on a cushion with fine scarlet embroidering, said to him: "I want to have more than just a fling with you, I find you attractive, I admire you, but I'm not going to give in to you, not while you're still in love with Laila; we'd have sex once or twice, then you'd soon abandon me, men are like that, and you are no exception, you don't love me—yet. Yet. Yet!" Majnun agreed, but then saw that Carmen started to run to Laila's side, and he, victorious, accompanied them, running, panting and pleased, under rice which was raining down from the windows of a large apartment building.

A little after noon, when the arrival to Madrid was announced, the sight outside the window looked like the Central Plain of Brazil, the same aridity, the same yellow color of the wispy, creeping vegetation. It was August 15th 2011, a Monday. The World Youth Day events were to start the following day and would last until the 21st. There was already talk of the next one, which would take place in Rio almost two years later, at the end of July.

As soon as he got reception on his iPhone, Majnun checked his email, among them one from Laila: "Better to turn yourself in." Turn himself in for what? And another from his grandfather: "The police are looking for you. I suggest you turn yourself in, my son." Had the dream he'd had the night before leaving for Madrid been real? One thing was certain: fortunately, the bullets hadn't hit his grandpa Dario. He bemoaned the fact that his grandpa had annoyed him so much recently, but recognized that no one but him had given shape to his character; he was his grandfather with a young body and spirit, adapted to these new times. He looked at his reflection in his iPhone: he had some of his grandpa's features.

He tried to remember, and now he was certain. He had, in fact, left his house that night. He really had stood watch in front of Laila's house, spying. He could only recall it with difficulty, but he remembered it. He remembered that it was dark. Remembered that he felt cold. Remembered a red car. Remembered a tall man with big ears getting out of it. Remembered, indeed, shooting at that man. Remembered that the man fell, that blood flowed on the ground below. Finally, he remembered that he, Majnun, ran along the highway, at night, fleeing, fleeing, fleeing, not knowing if he'd ever arrive anywhere. Remembered . . . And maybe he'd never even loaded the gun; none of that stuff had ever happened. Maybe he didn't even exist, maybe the world itself didn't exist, there was no mass in the universe, the stars didn't exist, nor planets, nor people . . .

"The Pope is arriving on the 18th," said Suzana, freeing him from his thoughts and his iPhone.

At least ten other young people wearing the yellow Brazilian national soccer jersey got off the plane with them. Contrary to what Majnun had anticipated, passport control was minimal. Lucky, he thought, hoping they'd continue having the same good luck throughout the trip.

They took the metro from the airport to Bilbao station. From there they walked—Majnun and Carmen with backpacks on their backs, Suzana rolling the four wheels of her suitcase along the sidewalk—to the Hostal Dos de Mayo, in Malasaña.

"The 'La movida' movement started here," said Majnun.

He told them that decades had already passed since the time of the radical aesthetics of the new wave, which was not just one wave, but many. The youth movement wanted to reinvent their culture once the Franco dictatorship was over. It was a movement of sex, drugs, and artistic creation, the catharsis of the youth, Majnun said, recalling his grandpa Dario's commentaries about May of '68 and the prognostications of his other grandpa, Sérgio, about the Middle East.

Despite its name, the *hostal* wasn't on the Plaza Dos de Mayo, but a few streets below it, heading towards Chueca.

Suzana complained about the heat at every opportunity.

"I'm not staying here," she said in protest at having to carry her suitcase up the stairs of the guesthouse.

"Set it down, I'll carry it," said Majnun, who then carried Suzana's suitcase to their room on the fourth floor.

They had barely settled in when Carmen had to leave. She had arranged to meet up with her friend Pablo that very afternoon.

Suzana crouched down to unpack her suitcase. Majnun, sitting on the edge of the bed, stared at the groove between the two plump flanks of her beautiful ass, as well as the top of her flesh-colored lace panties.

She turned on her iPod and tried out the small speaker she'd taken from her suitcase. When a hip-hop song came on, she started to move her shoulders and hips, her navel visible. Majnun followed suit. Then he started to accompany the rhythm of the song with handclaps and foot-stomps, like a flamenco dancer.

During the next hip-hop song, which he recognized as a remix of Missy Elliot's "Hot" by Ratatat, they were dancing as if they were out at a club, and Majnun could pick out a few sexy phrases from the song lyrics, which he imagined coming out of Suzana's mouth:

Show that DJ *how I shake my breast . . .*
Tight jeans, crop shirts, short skirts . . .
Got guns, so what, I ain't scurred . . .
I'm really, really hot . . .

When he put his hands on Suzana's hips, she said:
"No, that's enough," and turned off the music.

Cheers, I drink to that

Early the next morning, August 16th, a Tuesday, Suzana again played some music on her computer.

"'Cheers, I drink to that,'" said Majnun, raising an empty cup in Suzana's direction.

A Rihanna song was playing: "Yeah yeah / yeah yeah / yeah yeah / yeah yeah / yeah yeah / Don't let the bastards get ya down / Turn it around with another round / There's a party at the bar everybody put your glasses up and I drink to that / I drink to that / And I drink to that / I drink to that / And I drink to that."

After a long while in the bathroom, Suzana came out with a gold earring in one ear, a ring on her finger, a bracelet, cutoff jean shorts, and a violet T-shirt. From her large breasts emanated a perfume that made Majnun suffer.

"Is that to remember the passion of Christ?" Majnun asked, transforming, out of bashfulness, the praise he wanted to give into criticism.

She didn't reply.

It was risky to communicate via email with Laila, even if he changed his name and email address, but even so he asked, suspecting he already knew the answer: "Why are the police looking for me?"

Shit, he had shot that revolver. There had already been instances of him walking around the house at night and doing things that he didn't remember afterwards. And if they found the revolver under the cashew tree? And if Interpol sent orders to Spain?

In 2013, when Pope Francis was set to arrive in Rio de Janeiro for yet another World Youth Day, bringing with him the promise of a new spring for the Church, and Majnun ran into Suzana at a demonstration in Brasília, he remembered that day in Madrid, back in August 2011, on which he registered for Youth Day along with Suzana. At the center of the gathering, in the Plaza de San Juan de la Cruz, near the Nuevos Ministerios metro station, Suzana and Majnun each received a backpack, a copy of the Gospels, and *The Pilgrim's Book*, which detailed all the ceremonies. They also received the *Youth Day Guide*, with the program and schedule of cultural activities, the catechism *YouCat* or *Youth Catechism*, written for the youth with a prologue by the Pope, and a pass that gave them free access to all the cultural activities. If they wanted to confess — a volunteer informed them — there would be a "Festival of Forgiveness," with hundreds of participating priests in confessionals set up in Buen Retiro Park. Since Majnun had registered for the meal plan, he received food vouchers that would be accepted — according to what was explained to him — in over a thousand restaurants around the entire city. One of them was close by, on Calle Fernández de la Hoz.

They headed that way. The clock read two in the afternoon, and the thermometer, thirty-four degrees Celsius. The dryness of the air and the heat, combined with the warm wind out on the sidewalk, provoked in Majnun the odd sensation of reliving a dramatic moment from his childhood; the day on which his mother hid underneath the table, shaking, panicked, scared that she was being followed, as he was at that moment. He had also had spells of paranoia. Is that what was this was? A new spell? No, this situation was concrete. The emails he'd received were proof enough. The police were after him, maybe even the police in Madrid, who might have already been alerted.

"I can't stand this heat," said Suzana. "And I think I'm going to find a new hotel. The air conditioning at this one is no good. But you two don't have to worry, if I move to a different one, I'll still pay my part of this one."

They looked at the menu and chose some *tapas* and dishes to share: duck liver pâté, artichokes, Padrón peppers, Iberian ham, rice with squid, and lamb skewers with mushrooms.

"I love artichokes," said Suzana.

She talked nonsense, but nonsense from an enchanting face acquired a semblance of intelligence. She had refined table manners. With her back straight, she held her arms close to her body, while handling the fork and knife with precision and an economy of gesture. After they'd finished the food, she ordered a *cortado*. Then took a cigarette from her purse.

"You really don't want to see the Pope?" she asked.

"What I want to do is join up with the protestors, the *indignados*."

"Well we're going to keep different schedules. I don't understand anything about the *botellón*. I'd rather sit down in a nice air-conditioned restaurant."

Majnun thought about explaining that the protestors didn't have anything to do with the *botellón* drinking culture. He merely said:

"*Botellón no es revolución*."

"I need to do some shopping," announced Suzana. "Want to come with?"

"Where?"

"The Salamanca neighborhood."

"I'll go," he said resolutely, not because he was interested in shopping, but because it was pleasing to look at Suzana in a pair of tight shorts.

He soon regretted it. He'd gotten ahead of himself. His expression had betrayed him to Suzana, she certainly had read his mind, or at least his eyes, which didn't know how to hide their sensual pleasure. A mistake inside a larger mistake: that of having traveled to Madrid with Suzana.

"Let's go then," she said, getting up, a cigarette and a lighter in her hands. "Can you carry this for me?" she asked, pointing to her backpack.

Majnun slung a backpack over each shoulder, and they headed to the Salamanca neighborhood. He was unsure how to interpret the looks she gave in his direction. Critical looks. Perhaps she felt annoyed at having to walk beside such an awkward guy.

"My oh my oh my, what heat. I can't take it. You should wear a hat or at least put on some sunscreen," she said, exhaling puffs of smoke.

He stopped in front of a building and spoke, but very unnaturally, as if he had rehearsed the words in order to impress her:

"This is marvelous. Look at this door. I wonder what style this is.

There's nothing like this in Brasilia."

How nice it would have been to take that walk with Laila! She would have known better how to appreciate his taste.

He looked down at his phone a number of times to check the time, not because he wanted to know what time it was, but as a simple nervous tick. The fifth time he did it, Suzana asked:

"Do you have something planned? If you don't want to do this, you don't need to . . ."

"Me, something planned?" he laughed, awkwardly snapping out of his distracted state.

"You're not enjoying the stroll."

Why didn't he just spell it out, that he was missing Laila? That he wished she were there instead of Suzana?

Along the Paseo de la Castellana, shielded from the cruel sun by rows of trees, other young women with exposed legs walked along with a merely insinuated sensuality, different from what he was used to seeing in Brasilia. This was their Eixão, their main thoroughfare, with the difference that on their sidewalks and, above all, on their wide central promenade there was a constant movement of pedestrians. Cities had personality, imposed certain styles of behavior and dress. Even styles of walking, talking, and gesticulating.

Everything there looked different from Brasilia. It must have been the contrast between the new and the old, between a country with no memory and one that was molded by the weight of tradition. What about corruption? Did they have that here as well? He wasn't going to talk about this subject in front of Suzana, whose father was a friend of a federal deputy who had recently been indicted and was also an old friend of his grandpa Dario. "It's nothing but slander, the press condemns before they get their facts straight," had been the words of Grandpa Dario, whose critical opinions couldn't overcome that old friendship with his hometown friend and former schoolmate. "It's the people's fault. If you want to end corruption, you have to vote for people who are worth their salt," replied his grandma Elvira, whose opinions were always expressed as if they were water about to burst the dike.

"The protestors, the *indignados*, debate about everything. That's democracy. The 15-M movement wants to take back the squares that they only stopped occupying because of the police. If they start camping out again, I'm going to camp with them," said Majnun.

"The 15-M?"

"It started on May 15th. It's a movement, mainly made up of young people, against the immorality of the financial system, in favor of more transparency in political parties, changes in electoral law . . . But they aren't tied to ideologies or any organization . . . They use social networks and unite everyone who wanted to protest because of the crisis."

When they got to the Salamanca neighborhood, Suzana sat down on a sidewalk bench, welcoming the afternoon sun on her face. Majnun sat down beside her and they stayed there for a few minutes in silence, Majnun looking at the facades of the buildings, thinking about Laila.

"I know you're not the least bit interested. But I know everything around here, the stores and their prices. I came here with my parents last year."

Paying no mind to her gesture, Majnun took his phone out of his pocket once again, as if to check the time.

"You can't get your girlfriend off your mind, can you?" asked Suzana, noticing his blank expression.

Her comment surprised him. Had Carmen spoken with her about Laila?

"No," he replied, giving her a melancholic smile.

"Stop worrying about it so much. I'm telling you this for your own good."

"Then will you help me get her off my mind?"

"How?"

"You know how."

"No, I don't know, and if it's what I'm thinking, you can kiss that idea goodbye."

"You're the one who thought it. I wasn't going to go that far."

"Far where?"

"You guessed how I was feeling. That's my fault. I never am where I really am. My head's always somewhere else."

"Let's go," she said, getting up and offering her arm to him in a maternal gesture, like an adult looking after a small child. "Shopping and then off to the Prado, which is still open."

He took Suzana's hand, and they held hands for two blocks, their obedient eyes taking in the window displays on either side of the street.

"You'd look good in that shirt," said Suzana, in front of the window of a menswear shop.

"I can't buy anything, my backpack is already stuffed," he said apologetically.

Then, at a window display on Calle Claudio Coello, Suzana spotted a blue polka-dotted dress.

"What do you think?" she asked.

"Pretty."

"I'm going to try it on."

He liked it when, after looking at herself in the mirror, she paraded around for him, turning her body to one side and the other so that he could see her from all sides.

"Beautiful," he said, sincerely.

After the purchase, they headed to the Prado Museum, where Majnun leisurely examined every detail of *The Garden of Earthly Delights*, the triptych by Bosch, and attentively stared at the naked, voluminous body of Susanna as depicted under the concupiscent gaze of old men in the biblical scene from the Old Testament in the 1617 paintings by Guercino — Susanna nude with her back turned to the old men who devoured her with their eyes — then by Veronese, from 1580, in which she was covering her left breast with her hand, and by Tintoretto, from 1555, in which one of the old men was eagerly groping her right breast.

Little light of hope

That night he found underneath his pillow a knife covered in dark, dried, brittle blood. He rearranged the position of the pillow, under the impression that Carmen and Suzana were watching him. From Suzana's speaker, Bebel Gilberto was singing: "Our Lady is amazing / Our Lady is amazing . . ."

He went into the bathroom. When he returned, what a relief to find the knife was no longer there! Had Carmen or Suzana removed it? Were they going to turn him in? Or had it been a nightmare he'd had before even falling asleep?

"What happened, my friend?" asked Carmen. "You look pale. Come on, you can tell your friend," she said, hugging him.

"No, it's nothing."

The police finding him in Madrid was a long shot. He'd continue the trip as if nothing had happened. Above all, he wasn't going to say anything to Carmen or Suzana. He would leave all that worrying for when he returned to Brazil, if indeed he ever returned. Who knows, maybe from here he'd travel to Fez, following Boabdil's route? Or else to Tunis?

As soon as Carmen left the room, Suzana, starting to undress, commented:

"Dude, your beard has grown longer even since we arrived in Madrid."

Majnun's ears were deaf, though his eyes were fully functional, glued to the window and Suzana breasts. Her breasts were covered, but the window revealed a full moon, and unlike the stars, which literary types hold to be chaste, the moon had something lascivious and immoral about it; it aroused certain desires.

"Turn away from me," Suzana ordered.

The order served as an advertisement for what was in store for him to see: Suzana with her back to him, wearing a black G-string.

"I can't stand this heat," she said.

Then she went into the bathroom, the door to which didn't shut all the way—one advantage of cheap hotels. Through the crack in the doorjamb, Suzana's body, covered in soapsuds, was even more beautiful than he had imagined. She caressed her vulva with the bar of soap at length and, eyes closed, let the water run down her body. She carefully shaved her legs. With a pair of scissors, she trimmed what little pubic hair she had. She looked at herself in the mirror, cupping each breast in her hand. Majnun opened his fly and took out his hard cock.

She finally came out, wrapped in a towel. Once again she asked him to turn away from her. He saw her from behind, naked. There were no panties on the bed, just a nightgown made of transparent fabric. And now she might be completely naked under the bedsheet. Was it to arouse him? The music, the dancing, the bathroom, the naked body . . . None of it had been mere chance.

"And sex? Do you miss having sex?" he asked, aroused.

"Drop it. I'm not interested."

He imagined that Suzana was like a storefront display, protected by the glass; to be seen and admired, not touched. She wasn't chaste, she had never been any kind of Christian and was definitely open to certain intrusions, just not to him. She liked to be desired, to attract attention, yet she armed herself against inappropriate attacks. Physical contact: little of it and for the very few. Maybe he would have some luck with her?

"It's not a pickup line. Just curious."

"And why would I tell you about my private life?"

"I want to sleep with you," he said, sincere and direct, stroking his rigid penis under the sheet.

"Who do you think I am?"

"A charming young thing who's on vacation with me."

"No, I didn't come here on vacation with you. You're the one who wanted to come with me. And if I'd come here to have sex, it wouldn't be with you. Have you already forgotten about Laila?"

So, she even knew her name? Ah, Carmen, she couldn't keep a secret . . .

"Not even if you knew that I'm dying 'cause I'm so horny for you?"

"Doesn't seem like it. You can't keep your mind off of Laila. Forget about that *cougar*!" she said, pronouncing the English word "KOO-gare."

Majnun could only guess at the pejorative meaning of the word, but her response pleased him, since it left a door half-open for him. If he could show her that Laila didn't occupy all of his mind . . . He thought about uncovering himself to show her the desire he felt. And what if he confessed to the drama that was going on with Laila? No. Too complicated to explain that he wasn't a murderer, or worse, that perhaps he was.

"Nothing is more important in life than sex, don't you think?" he asked, still stroking himself underneath the sheet.

"I don't agree."

"What's more important, then?"

"Oh, a lot of things. Love, most of all."

He agreed. But his desire to learn, to change the world, to participate in great events, and to be with Laila all bowed down before that other, immediate desire, incited by the full moon and those two other moons, also full, of that naked body.

He didn't love Suzana; he only—and perhaps "only" wasn't the right word—desired her. It was electrifying to know that under that sheet she was wearing a transparent nightgown or was even completely naked.

"Do you have casual sex?"

"So nosy!"

"Have you ever?"

"There's no such thing as casual sex."

"With someone who you might not even want to see again afterwards."

"Since you really want to know," she said laughingly, with a laugh that was spontaneous and prideful, more prideful than spontaneous.

"What? Tell me."

"One time I got in a car wreck and went to see my insurance agent. That same day I received a phone call from a young guy at the insurance agency asking me to dinner. He was kind of an idiot, but I accepted."

"Why?"

"There was this attraction, to go out with a guy who was only physically attractive to me, a guy I didn't even know really."

"And isn't that a sin, Suzana?"

"You think Christians never sin? I'm not a slut. And I'm also not saying that we ended up going all the way."

"Even if it didn't happen then, it still could happen now."

"True. It could."

"Why not with me?"

"Ah, you think you're attractive, do you?"

"I know I'm no Brad Pitt."

"That's not why I wouldn't do it. It's because I wouldn't be able to face you again. I wouldn't know how to act the next time we ran into each other."

"But it's all the same anyway. We're strangers."

"And you think I want to have sex with some random stranger? You're not a stranger."

"Then sex with a friend. Why not?"

"Because no."

"If you don't want me, I'll kill myself."

"Then kill yourself. Your computer is more important to you than I am. Sometimes I think that if we tossed all your computers in the trash, you'd be able to get more out of this trip."

Her comments lit a little light of hope. So that was it? She was jealous of his computers?

"If I destroy this iPad, will you love me?"

"That's so monumentally stupid, comparing me to an iPad. Plus, you'd never be able to do it."

"Watch, then."

He raised the iPad and gestured with it, as if he were going to throw it to the other side of the room.

"Stop being such a fool."

He perceived something tender in her words. He got up. He was wearing nothing but briefs, through which the shape of his hard cock was visible. He rifled through his backpack, looking for a pencil and his notebook. Then he wrote: "Suddenly, a body on fire searching for another body to set ablaze." He put the piece of paper in one of the pockets of the backpack, a substitute for his shoebox.

"I can't find what I want on the internet," Majnun said, standing in front of his computer.

"What?"

"I want to read more about the Muslims in Spain, the ones of Eastern origin and the ones from West Africa. I've found a lot of scattered information here and there, but I want something more detailed. I know that, among those from the east, the Arabs considered themselves direct descendants of the Prophet Mohammed, and thus saw themselves as a pure race. But the ones from West Africa, the Moors, were better warriors. There was a rivalry between them for control of Muslim Spain."

"You mean that those people have been fighting among themselves since way back then?"

They felt the wall vibrate. It was coming from the room next door. They could hear screams, moaning.

"Don't worry, I think they're just having some fun over there," said Majnun.

"Yeah, you're right," said Suzana, laughing as they heard more moaning and felt the wall shaking harder.

Majnun tried to concentrate on his reading. He read more about the Abencerrages, whom Washington Irving called an oriental race. During the time of the fall of Granada, they had remained loyal to their faith and their Muslim king. They disappeared, unlike those who surrendered to the conquering Catholics and were rewarded with high posts and lands and became noblemen for all posterity, like the Venegas family.

"I feel sympathy for the Abencerrages," said Majnun, who noticed that Suzana had fallen asleep, the volume of her body well-outlined underneath the white sheet.

Time for outrage!

It was a Thursday, August 17th, late afternoon, and various Catholic ceremonies that Suzana, as well as Majnun, had attended had come to a close. Suzana downloaded new songs from iTunes and played them loud while she took the blue dress with white polka dots that she'd purchased at a shop on Calle Claudio Coello the day before out of its bag. As if seeing a series of photographs, Majnun remembered her in the dress, looking at herself in the mirror, then turning from one side to another in front of him.

Maria Gadú was singing: "I don't have time to say your name / I don't have a name for you to speak ... / If Shiva tells me to be patient / I'll grab you in the alley of the bell of belief / I'll scare you with the wrath of my madness ..."

Later, Suzana started to sway to the rhythm of a song in English. "Erykah Badu, 'Love,'" she said.

Majnun listened, thinking about Laila. Laila wasn't crude like Suzana. He didn't merely feel physical desire for her, but rather a thirst that came from the soul and spread to his guts: "Come on, feel me / Just tell me you love me, I like it, you know it / So do it, come on, come on ... / Baby, baby, I'm about to go insane ..."

He didn't receive a reply from Laila to the email he'd sent the day before. The death of her husband had certainly shaken her. It shouldn't have. Majnun had seen with his own eyes the bruises on her body put there by that monster.

Majnun searched the internet for news about the murder of Laila's husband. There were several murders in the Brasilia newspapers — in Lago, in Plano Piloto, in Guará, in Taguatinga, in Ceilândia, in Núcleo Bandeirante, in Samambaia, and in other satellite cities ... Finally, a homicide at a lakefront home in Asa Norte. The victim was getting out of his car when he was struck by four bullets. He was survived by a widow, no children. Investigations were underway.

Carmen commented:

"Did you know that here in Madrid, and only during World

Youth Day, excommunication can be lifted for those who had abortions? And there are also plenary indulgences for Youth Day volunteers."

"Have you two ever had an abortion?" asked Majnun, putting on his black shirt, which fit tight against his fragile body.

"What a question!" protested Suzana.

"Why do you want to know?" asked Carmen.

"Well you don't even have to tell me, I can already tell," said Majnun.

"You're the one drawing conclusions."

When they left the room, they came across two tall, muscular men. Their neighbors.

"Were they the ones making all that noise yesterday?" mused Majnun.

"What noise?" asked Carmen.

"The wall was shaking," replied Suzana, miming a sarcastic, silent laugh with a movement of her eyes and lips.

The laughter exploded and took over her entire face, forced her to close her eyes and made her body tremble. She went back to the room; she had forgotten her cell phone.

It was eight o'clock at night, still light out, and Carmen and Majnun went down to the lobby to wait for the arrival of Pablo, Carmen's friend.

"I saw Professor Rodrigo yesterday, Pablo's dad," said Carmen. "He's giving a lecture on Monday about jihad and other Islamic subjects. He asked about you."

Then she added, quietly, as if someone might overhear her:

"Don't worry, he knows nothing."

As always, Carmen knows everything, thought Majnun.

Pablo arrived and, because of his height, had to bend down to kiss Carmen's forehead. Then he softly ran his hands along the back of her white dress, made of cool, fine linen. He was, at most, twenty-five years old. He was muscular and of a ruddy complexion, with rosy cheeks that contrasted with his lively black eyes, as well as his thick eyebrows and goatee, also black. As he showed Majnun his extremely straight teeth in an exaggerated smile and shuffled his Havaiana brand sandals with little Brazilian flags on them—a present from Carmen—he conveyed an easygoing air.

Examining that walking Greek sculpture, whose muscles were visible underneath his red T-shirt, Majnun discerned a certain elegance, even down to the sandals. He felt like a slob in shorts that went halfway down his shin and worn out sneakers. He tried to straighten up his polo shirt and his thoughts. The pause before greeting the Spaniard served to recompose his confidence and erase his feelings of inferiority.

Pablo firmly shook Majnun's hand and, in his baritone voice, said it was a pleasure to finally meet him. Then he pulled Carmen aside, as if to tell her a secret. While they waited for Suzana, Majnun leafed through a few days' newspapers that were lying on a table near the hotel entrance.

When she came down the stairs, Pablo's eyes roamed across her tight, cutoff jean shorts, the same ones she'd worn the day before, and her white blouse, through which her bra was visible. Majnun knew that he shouldn't be jealous, but it's one thing to know and another entirely to feel. Did this Adonis with well-groomed hair want to monopolize all the women? Let him have Carmen, in that case. Just her. But he didn't even like the idea of Pablo being with Carmen. Jealousy? He didn't know what to call the feeling of not allowing another person to want someone that he didn't even want himself.

"Look at this news: they lowered the USA's credit rating," said Majnun, thinking that Suzana, an economics major, would be interested in the story.

"And what does that have to do with us?" she replied.

Majnun then showed them some advertisements in the newspaper that were accompanied by silhouettes of women: "Ladies in your city, depraved, young, mature, married, single, hot, adventurous, perverted."

"Have at it. If that's what you want . . ." said Carmen.

"Let's go to the protest against the Pope, *vale*?" suggested Pablo.

"I want to make it clear that I'm not on board with anything you all are planning," explained Suzana. "It's disrespectful for you to come here during Youth Day," she said, looking at Majun, "and, on top of not participating in anything, you're going to join the protests."

"*Venga*, it's just that it's a waste of money, even public funds," explained Pablo.

"That's a lie. Youth Day helps your economy," Suzana rejoindered sternly, unable to hide her animosity.

"One of Spain's problems is that the Catholic Church has too much power. A consequence of the so-called *reconquista*. Suffice it to say that it was the only religion with legal status until 1976," insisted Pablo.

They left the *hostal* by a side street, heading towards the Calle del Almirante.

"You can't complain about me," said Majnun, walking beside Suzana and whispering in her ear. "You knew that I didn't come here for World Youth Day, but today I took part in almost the entire program. And you aren't anything like those Youth Day people either. Admit it, you didn't come to see the Pope. You came to go shopping."

"Don't insult me," she said angrily, moving away from him.

They continued along the Calle de Gravina, crossed the Plaza de Chueca, walked up Calle Augusto Figueroa, and came upon a large crowd when they arrived at Calle Fuencarral. Several young women, carrying signs that said "Abolish Bullfighting" above a picture of a bleeding bull, were wearing T-shirts printed to look bloody. Majnun noted that the red on the T-shirts was lighter-colored than the blood on the knife he'd found under his pillow the night before.

"Do Spaniards still like bullfights?" he asked Pablo, imagining himself as some sort of Hemingway.

"People my age like it less and less, but it's still one of the biggest sports. *Venga*, if you read the newspaper today, you'll find a story about a bull named Mouse—ten years old and five hundred pounds—who has claimed another victim. He's already killed two and injured several others. Because of that, he's the most sought-after bull at the festivals in Valencia. That animal's appearance fee has gone through the roof. It costs two thousand euros to rent a bull for a festival, but people pay ten thousand for Mouse to make an appearance at a festival for less than an hour. He has his own website, and it seems like the owner wants to clone him. On the other hand, starting in September, bullfights will no longer be permitted in Catalonia. A 300 year-old tradition coming to a close."

"I was born on a ranch in the *sertão* region of Ceará, and when I was little I saw a lot of sheep slaughtered with a blow to the head. The animal would convulse, hanging upside down, tied up by its feet. The meat would still be trembling when they removed the skin," said Carmen.

They made their way through the multitude of young people wearing backpacks on Fuencarral Street, heading towards the Puerta del Sol. As they crossed the Gran Vía on Calle de la Montera, several prostitutes were out on the prowl.

"Just look at where you all are taking me. It's so filthy here," objected Suzana, pointing at papers that had been tossed on the ground.

"When there's no rain, filth starts to accumulate," explained Pablo.

It was nine at night, still light out, and the protest against the Pope—who was set to arrive the following day, August 18th—was gaining momentum. As they neared the Puerta del Sol, they saw a confrontation between some young people and the police.

"This way, people! Take some of these signs," ordered Majnun.

And what if he went to jail because of the protest? He'd very quickly be identified as the person who murdered Laila's husband. But for that very reason he needed to face his fear, like someone jumping off the top of a cliff into the sea.

Suzana yelled out, in a Brazilian accent, towards the protestors: "*¡Viva el Papa! ¡Somos la juventud del Papa!*"

No reaction.

At ten o'clock the police started to shut down the protest and drive everyone out of the Puerta del Sol.

Majnun picked up two signs off the ground. One of them read: "Ratzinger's a liar, Christ would have gone to Somalia"; the other: "No More Church Privilege. Equality!"

"If they catch you, you're going to get deported," warned Suzana.

Once again, he suspected that Suzana might know something. Had she seen the knife the night before? Had she received news from Brasilia about the suspicions swirling around him? Had Carmen told her something?

They walked down Calle de Alcalá. Suzana wanted to go into the Church of the Calatravas.

"Just to see it," she explained.

Majnun accompanied her. He admired the lavish interior of the church, its circular cupola, its elegant columns, the gilded and polychrome wooden altar in a Churrigueresque baroque style. He noticed a painting of Saint Raimundo de Fitero, founder of the Calatrava Order, surrounded by the spoils of war, as well as a sculpture of the Immaculate Conception.

A priest cast a disdainful look at Suzana's outfit as he walked out of the church.

"The history of this church is connected to the Military Order of Calatrava, which was created to fight against the Muslims," said Pablo informatively.

"Now where are we going to go?" inquired Carmen.

"If we head right from here, we can get dinner at Casa Manolo, near Zarzuela Theater."

"I'm not hungry. Why don't we head down to the Paseo de Recoletos?" suggested Suzana.

They walked between the trees that lined the Paseo de Recoletos.

"We can keep going until we get to Calle del Almirante and find a *tapas* bar around there."

Suzana insisted that they find a bar somewhere along Castellana. They initially sat down at a table out on the patio, but Suzana couldn't stand the heat and quickly convinced them to go inside where there was air conditioning.

"*Cuatro cañas*," ordered Pablo, after confirming that everybody wanted a draft beer.

They conversed about recent films and singers that had emerged in Brazil and the United States in the last few years.

"I wanted to be an *indignado* protestor like you guys here. There's such enormous passivity in Brazil," Majnun told Pablo at one point in the conversation.

"*Venga*, the thing is that you all don't have the problem we have, what with half of young people unemployed. We study hard here and then can't find a job. We're *pre-parados*: prepared and pre-pared down."

"I'm unemployed too," argued Majnun.

"Jobs for fiction writers don't exist," said Carmen.

"I defend the right to idleness and a salary, not to employment and work. It's not unemployment that's bad, it's not having a salary. A job is just a means to gaining idleness and pleasure," said Majnun, gesturing excitedly and stroking his beard.

"You don't really think that," said Carmen. "You're the most idealistic person I know."

"Spain's problem isn't only a problem with Spain. Everything is interconnected. What happens here is mirrored throughout the entire world," said Pablo. "*Pues nada*, we need a global change, a change in structure, in everything. It's of no use if you only try to change one country."

Suzana complained about the dryness of the air, which was making her nose bleed. She excused herself to go to the restroom.

Outside, visible through the restaurant windows, backpackers were walking down the tree-lined street.

"And what are the demands of the movement?" Majnun asked Pablo. "I read that the name was inspired by a pamphlet written by a ninety-three-year-old man . . ."

"*Indignez-vous* or 'Time for Outrage,' by Stéphane Hessel. The slogan of the French Resistance. For him, the worst thing is indifference, we should be like the yeast that makes the bread rise. *Venga*, it's up to us if this is going to be a society we can be proud of, not one that's suspicious of immigrants and cuts spending on social security, welfare, healthcare, and education."

Later, still talking to Majnun, Pablo said:

"Carmen told me about your Spanish grandfather who lived in Lebanon."

"My paternal grandfather, Sérgio, who lives in São Paulo. But, no, he isn't Spanish, just a descendant of Spaniards."

"I'm getting up early tomorrow. The Pope's going to be here," said Suzana as she returned to the table.

"But the night's just getting started here in Madrid," objected Pablo. "I propose we keep this going at a café in the Plaza del Humilladero or over on Calle Cava Baja, in La Latina."

"No, I don't want to get to bed late," said Suzana.

"We can go somewhere closer, buy some beers from a *latero* and get in on the *botellón* in the Plaza de San Ildefonso. You guys will like it."

"I'm in," said Carmen.

What did they do, she and Pablo, during all that time they spent together? Majnun felt like something was going to happen between them, if there wasn't already something going on. They laughed for no reason, talked endlessly amongst themselves. About what? And why did it bother him?

Since Suzana insisted on going back to the guesthouse, he went with her, not because he wanted to catch a glimpse of the Pope in the middle of a huge crowd the next day, but because, drunk on beer and hope, he intended on seeing Suzana in the intimacy of their room that night.

A chapter that promises torrid scenes, which aren't a reason to skip it, especially since a promise is neither fact nor debt

"Turn away from me," Suzana told him once more, just after they had entered the room.

This time Majnun had no doubt: she was doing it on purpose. Suzana went into the bathroom loosely wrapped in a sheet, maybe even naked underneath that sheet. He recalled the paintings from the Prado Museum, and the real Suzana started to take on the forms of the Suzanas in those paintings. Then she transformed into the young woman loosely wrapped in a sheet, contemplating a skull, like on the postcard that Laila had sent him. Bad premonition. Sign of danger.

He took off his briefs. When she came out of the bathroom, he went over to her.

"No," she screamed.

Majnun violently threw her onto the bed, both of them naked, struggling against each other.

"I'm a virgin," she said.

Feigned protestation, he thought. He turned her over on her belly, pulling her towards the corner of the bed.

Let's skip the details.

"You pig," she repeated. "You brute. That was rape," she said, crying. "You raped me, you son of a bitch."

"No. I just tried to."

"Never speak to me again," she said, crying.

And then more and more tears ran down her face, some tears of hate, others of humiliation, others of rage at herself for having allowed such a thing to happen, even though it didn't happen.

While she went into the bathroom, naked, in order to wash off her back, he wrote down on a scrap of paper: "joy and sadness sleep in the same bed." Then he tossed the paper into his backpack.

"Get out of here," she said as she came back from the bathroom, wrapped in a towel.

"Where to?"

"To hell. You're certainly not staying here."

"Weren't you the one who wanted to change hotels?"

She grabbed a sandal and threw it as hard as she could at his face, which seemed to him a form of tenderness, like when she called him a fool.

She put the towel aside and covered herself with a sheet.

"I'm being serious. Get the hell out of my life," she said in tearful screams.

"I'm sorry, it's just that you're . . ."

He thought of various slang terms that denoted lust, but opted for more sensible words.

"You're beautiful," he said, completing the phrase, his voice smothered by regret.

"Stop. Enough, you bastard!"

It was the same name that Laila's husband had called him.

"If you knew . . ."

"I know. And I'm not interested. Shoo, you coward!"

She was right. He was an utter nobody, a piece of shit, a bastard.

"I'm going to disappear. You'll never see me again."

"Great. Can't happen soon enough."

The wall started to shake. It must have been the couple next door again, two muscular men pounding the bed against the wall like a pile driver. This time Majnun couldn't manage a smile, nor did Suzana show any sign that she could even hear it.

He walked along the narrow sidewalks, stepping over puddles of dog piss and piles of dog shit. Why did he feel crushed, when he should have felt proud of his boldness?

Suzana was definitely going to tell Carmen. Then Carmen would say to him: "Majnun, I thought so highly of you. Now I know what you are: a bastard." What shame! He really was an idiot. Why couldn't he understand women? Suzana would complain to her parents, the news would spread throughout Brasilia, get back to his grandpa Dario, his grandma Elvira, and even his beloved grandma Mona . . . From one telling to the next it would get exaggerated, he'd be exposed as a degenerate, a sexual aggressor . . . And Laila? Would she ever forgive him?

The desire was real, he had to admit it. He didn't love Suzana, he was certain of that, but he felt so horny! He only hadn't shown it before out of shyness. Ever since he watched her unpack her suitcase on the day they arrived in Madrid, he had woken up in the middle of the night thinking about her. Or, more precisely, about her body; or, better still, about certain details of her body. And then he would start mentally caressing her in those parts. And not just caress her. He had naively thought that those mental exercises would be enough to calm his senses.

What he'd done was serious, he understood that. The person who attacked Suzana wasn't him; or, on the contrary, who knows, perhaps that was his true self, lascivious and confused. He saw a *tapas* bar with the facade of an old pharmacy: *azulejo* tiles with blue borders and yellow background on either side of the door, depicting a man in a tie on one side and a woman in a long green dress on the other, both of them promoting medicines. He went in, not knowing what he wanted. He uttered some senseless phrases in Portuguese, managing in the middle to stammer out, with lips quaking, the word "*vino*," which was brought to him time and again. He drank until he'd finished off the correct and necessary dose for numbness, anesthesia for the soul of a person who needed to keep walking through the streets without knowing where he was going.

He was panting, he had difficulty breathing, and his heart was pounding. Should he go back to the hotel? Get down on his knees and apologize to Suzana? Kiss her feet? For a fraction of a second he had a feeling that Carmen would protect him. No, he had no future. Everything was lost. Better that the police find him, try him, and toss him into prison, where his life would gain meaning. He turned off his cell phone so he wouldn't be bothered.

Tipsy, he felt a shiver despite the heat, perhaps the beginnings of a fever. Where was he walking? He had already passed this street coming from the other direction. Was he walking in circles around the same city block? In a triangular park, with tables out on the sidewalk, joyful people with beers and glasses of wine gesticulated endlessly. Was he lost? No. He just had to follow the flow, go where other people were going.

Was it dangerous to take the deserted, dark streets that attracted him the most? He soon found another flood of people and cars. What time was it? He recognized the Gran Vía, which he walked down, following a group of young people, maybe all Muslims, since the woman in the middle was covered with a burka. He reached the Plaza de Cibeles, from where he could see the Puerta de Alcalá. Minutes later he entered Buen Retiro Park, remembering that this was where the "Festival of Forgiveness" was taking place. That was what he needed, forgiveness. Would he see Suzana there?

He walked passed the lake, turned left, and arrived at a promenade of white confessionals, sharp-edged shapes pointing towards the sky like the tail of an airplane. By his estimate, more than two hundred confessionals. But it was late, there were no priests around, the "Festival of Forgiveness" had ended, he wouldn't be forgiven today.

He took a path to the right which soon curved further to the right. He picked up the pace along the deserted path, turned right again, and walked along another wide, poorly lit promenade.

He saw a sign for the Palacio de Cristal. Along the way, a young woman in a long-sleeved shirt, sitting on a bench, smiled at him. Was he attracting attention?

The Palacio de Cristal was closed. He checked out the interior through the glass doors. The exhibit, entitled "To Be Continued," was by an artist who was born in Sarajevo, Maja Bajevic. Did it have something to do with the 15-M protests? There was a reference to Walter Benjamin, one of his theses about the philosophy of history, specifically Thesis V. He sat down on one of the steps outside the building. A quick Google search yielded this sentence: "The true image of the past escapes us, for the past is an image that sparkles for a moment, then quickly disappears."

He got up and put his face up against one of the glass doors of the Palacio. He saw what appeared to be scaffolding, part of the exhibit, and, on top of it, words written on a plate of glass covered in dust. It was an installation called "Performance/Random Category." The words were ephemeral, soon to be erased so that others could be written. Majnun was able to make out a quote from Antonio Machado: "Uncertain, indeed, is the future, for who knows what will happen? But uncertain, too, is the past, for who knows what has happened?"

He went back along the same route. Would the young woman still be there? Was she still sitting on the bench? Would she smile at him again?

Now, accompanied by two other young women, also dressed in long-sleeved shirts, she was talking with a young man in blue workout clothes. Majnun passed slowly beside them and looked at the young woman, who didn't notice him. She was concentrating on the conversation, which was in English:

"So, have you read *The Book of Mormon*?"

"Yes, I have, but . . ."

The inquisitor moon and the tragic novella

Again arriving at the lake, he saw people on the other side of it sitting on the steps of the Monument to Alfonso XII. He headed over there. Feeling the warm breeze on his face, he was moved by the moon shimmering on the water. The trees beyond were outlined against a pale gray sky, cloudless and with a tenuous light.

A group of young men—the same ones from before, minus one guy and the woman in the burka—were conversing in Arabic. He went over to them and greeted them, also in Arabic. The young men were friendly and kind, and their friendliness and kindness doubled in size when they found out he was from Brazil. They wanted to steer the conversation towards soccer, but Majnun didn't like soccer and hadn't yet started to follow the controversies surrounding the construction of the stadiums, as he would come to do in 2013.

One of the young men had a cousin in São Paulo and for a few years had thought about living in Brazil. They exchanged thoughts about São Paulo, a city that was growing more violent than Rio. The young man smiled, looking around at all the others and especially Majnun, the corners of his lips, bordered by a thin mustache, drawing back in a subtle, ironic manner.

Majnun tried to free himself from that provocative smile with a shameless question:

"Are you all Muslim?"

Yes, they all were. But they were all from different places. One was from Libya; another was from Morocco, a city in the north near Ceuta; the bearded guy with a skullcap was from the United States; and the curly-haired blonde guy was from Lebanon.

"Lebanon?"

Majnun then told them about his connections to Lebanon and Egypt on the side of his paternal grandparents.

"With this dude, it's his father who's from the Middle East," said the Libyan, pointing at the American.

"His dad was born in Yemen," said the Moroccan.

The American remained quiet and serious.

Majnun spoke about his grandma Mona and the conversations he'd had with her about Islam, including his possible conversion.

Finally, he broached the subject that especially interested him that night. If two young, unmarried people have sexual relations, would Allah forgive them?

"Allah isn't vengeful. He is tolerant, most wise, as it says in the Koran," said the grinning young man with the mustache, the Libyan, whose lips, disappearing into the sides of his face, still had a look of irony on them.

"Well, don't get the wrong idea. Under Sharia, it's as easy to get married as it is to get divorced. But sexual relations outside of marriage? Don't even think about it. Both people must die," said the bearded guy in the skullcap, in Arabic, and with a noticeable accent. He was the American, a tall guy, with a sunburned, masculine face marked by lateral wrinkles.

He had expressive eyes, full of pride and, it seemed to Majnun, integrity.

"Don't exaggerate, where does that happen?" asked the Libyan, who was the one with a cousin in São Paulo.

"It should happen everywhere, if the people are Muslim."

"Those are just your radical ideas."

"It's in the Koran."

"Not like that. And afterwards there has to be proof: four witnesses who have to have seen, truly seen, all of it, right down to the pen in the inkwell, as the ulama put it, which makes the rule impractical."

"In the case of adulterous women, there's no doubt, they should be stoned to death," argued the bearded guy in the skullcap, the American with the sunburned face.

"The Koran doesn't mention stoning, but rather one hundred lashes," explained the Libyan, "but even that doesn't make any sense in this day and age. For people who commit adultery, men and women, it says that they should be left in peace if they repent and change their ways."

"Those excesses exist in very few places, like Iran: death by stoning for adulterous women and ninety-nine lashes for those who have sexual relations outside of marriage," said the curly-haired, blonde Lebanese guy.

Majnun imagined that, aside from his attack on Suzana, if he were Muslim he would have committed another sin that night.

"Is drinking wine forbidden?" he asked.

"No, it's not. If you read the Book closely, you'll find that wine can be made and that it brings as many ill effects as benefits. Only excess is prohibited, which leads to intoxication," replied the Libyan.

"Actually, a verse from the Medinan *surahs* says that intoxicating drinks are the abominable handiwork of Satan," argued the American.

"Don't confuse the kid. Look, just because you like wine doesn't mean you can't convert," said the Libyan.

"And is there some rule about how to dress?" Majnun inquired, recalling his grandma Mona explaining that she didn't have to wear a veil.

"Look at us," said the Libyan. "This guy wears a skullcap because he likes it. Now, for women, yes . . ."

"But the faith has its rules about clothing, doesn't it? Because our outward behavior reveals the righteousness of the spirit. Happiness is in imitating Mohammed. Hence the obligation to wear a turban when one is standing," explained the American. "For women, the rule is very clear: they must conserve their modesty; they must cover their shoulders and breasts with their veils and must not show their attractive features to any man but their husbands, parents, in-laws, children, siblings . . ."

"Did you memorize that so you could control your girlfriend?" interrupted the Libyan.

"Modesty is a masculine virtue as well."

"Look who's talking! Where's your turban, dude?" contested the Libyan.

"I admit that I should be wearing one, even though I'm seated. I wear my skullcap in place of the turban for now. It's also important to start with the right foot when you're putting on your shoes."

"Why?" asked Majnun.

"It's what must be done so that the gates of happiness aren't closed for you," explained the tall guy with the beard, the American in the skullcap. "The same way that you must eat with your right hand and, when you're cutting your fingernails, start with the index finger of your right hand and end with the thumb of the right hand; and you must start with the pinky toe of your right foot and end with the pinky toe of your left foot."

Majnun noticed that those two, the Libyan and the bearded American, didn't see eye to eye. Were they from different sects? It seemed obvious that the bearded guy belonged to a militant group, maybe one of the ones he had visited on the internet. Since he thought it would be rude to ask directly, he introduced the subject subtly:

"I want to convert to Islam, like I said. But which Islam?"

"There is only one Islam," said the bearded guy.

"What I mean is: should I become a Sunni? Shiite? Ismaili? Sufi? Druze? Alawite? Salafi? Wahhabi? What difference does it make?"

"You're mixing things up here. Alawites are also Shiites. Ismailis, though they only recognize the first seven Shia imams and not all twelve, are Shiites. Salafis and Wahhabis are both Sunni," said the curly-haired Lebanese guy.

He explained that Sunnis and Shiites were divided on the question of succession of the Prophet. For the Shiites, the imams were the successors of Ali, Mohammed's cousin and son-in-law, as well as the fourth Caliph. Within Shia Islam, there were also disagreements regarding successors: the sixth imam, Ja'far al-Sadiq, designated his firstborn son, Ismael, as his successor, but, since he died before his father, the succession fell to his other son, Musa al-Kadhim, who is recognized as the true successor by the majority of Shiites. Others believed, however, that Ismael hadn't really died, he'd just hidden himself, and those people are his followers. That's why they're called Ismailis. They believe that Ismael will return at the end of days. They conceal their religion if they are forced to do so because of persecution, in order to safeguard and protect themselves—a practice that's based in the Koran.

The Moroccan, who had been quiet up to that point, suggested—with a profound look in his eyes and a soft voice— that Majnun should go to a certain community center, and started to give him the address. However, the Libyan immediately opposed this, advising Majnun that he shouldn't get involved with "that stuff." He suggested that he go to a mosque.

"Which mosque?" asked Majnun.

"Go to the mosque on the M-30, everyone knows where it is, and you'll be able to find it easily."

Lying on a bench in the park, using his backpack as a pillow and looking up at an inquisitor moon, Majnun fell asleep with the idea that his only salvation was in his novella. In it, there'd be a place for him, Suzana, Carmen, and Laila. To make those four characters unrecognizable—even him—he'd start by dressing them in their respective shawls and turbans, then transport them to the Middle Ages—more precisely, to Granada. He sprinkled in an Arabic word here and there to impress the reader. Made Suzana a Christian prisoner of the sultan, who would be Majnun himself, playing the role of Boabdil's father, Sultan Abul Hasan, the twenty-first and second-to-last sultan of Granada. Didn't he, Majnun, have a beard as thick as the sultan's? Wasn't he of equally low character, equally violent? Didn't he have a heart as hard as the sultan's? Wasn't it true that the sultan traded his wife, Fátima, for a Christian prisoner, Isabel de Solís, who became known as Soraya, just as he had unjustly traded Laila for Suzana? Suzana could be Soraya, the morning star, and with her Majnun would have two sons, Saab and Nasr, the same ones the sultan fathered with Soraya. But would it be right to compare Laila with Fátima, also known as Aixa al-Horra, the free, the honored, the honest? Laila was less virtuous and more beautiful than her, but everything fits in fiction. It would be especially fitting to describe himself as depraved. For hadn't Abu l-Hasan Ali once invited members of the court to watch Soraya bathe, then offered them each a saucer of the water in which she had bathed? Didn't he drink wine and smoke hashish at parties with female slaves? Wasn't it true that during the first thirteen centuries of the Hijri calendar, according to Sharia law, a man could buy female slaves and have sexual relations with them? That until the abolition of the caliphate by Ataturk in 1924, the caliphs had their own harems, "reserves" of hundreds or even thousands of women?

The novella would be realistic and tragic. Tragic for him, the main character, who would lose the war and the throne to his son. For Suzana, or Soraya, it would be the opposite: she would triumph after Boabdil's surrender to the Christians; she would again use her Christian name and baptize her two children, who would become the *infantes* of Granada, named Don Fernando and Don Juan.

Majnun felt that he deserved this tragic end. If he had never committed the execrable acts of the sultan, it was only because he wasn't a sultan, he lived in the twenty-first century, and Suzana wasn't his slave. He was as vile and human as evil itself, or perhaps he was evil itself.

He thought about jotting down these thoughts, adding this note: if he didn't modify the novella, he would be unjust to Laila, relegated to the role of an abandoned sultaness, and above all to Carmen, forgotten after the first few sentences. But he didn't write down a thing, because it was dark and he was already settled in and drowsy on that park bench.

Where are honor and dishonor?

Upon awaking to the brightness of the day, a Thursday, August 18th, when the Pope was perhaps already in the city, he noticed that the night before he had received another email from Laila on his iPhone: "there's no use hiding the police know that you bought the bullets."

What should he do? It wouldn't be an act of cowardice, but rather of courage, to leave them all behind—Laila, Carmen, Suzana, his grandparents—and disappear without a trace, continuing on to Africa or the Middle East to take part in a revolution. He would bet that that's what the bearded American was up to. Why hadn't he gotten his contact information?

He wasn't going to worry. Someday, if he ever returned to Brasilia, he would explain everything. But what if Interpol had an arrest warrant out on him?

Feeling restless, he strolled through the park and bought a paper hat made in China from a Sudanese *mantero*. Later he took care to slip away from the police car that was scaring away all the street vendors, including the Sudanese man. He left the park and had breakfast in a bakery on the Plaza de la Independencia.

He walked over to the Paseo del Prado and entered the Thyssen-Bornemisza Museum. He spent half an hour in front of a painting by Monet, *Charing Cross Bridge*, from 1899: an afternoon, light filtered through the winter fog, a few barges under the bridge, the silhouette of the Parliament building subtly visible in the background. He imagined throwing himself off that bridge and dissolving into that vague landscape.

"Suzana's right. It's horribly hot out," he thought as he left the museum. He took off his shirt, headed towards the Prado, then turned right, backpack on his shoulders, onto Calle de las Huertas, reading quotes from writers inscribed on the pavement as he went. He finally arrived at the Plaza de Santa Ana, surrounded by restaurants and beer halls full of people.

At a table in the middle of the square he ordered *una caña* and a *solomillo*, a pork loin, which came with potatoes. Could he commit himself, for religious reasons, to stop eating such delicious meat? He could even accept that "diet is the beginning of all cures," as the Prophet put it, but to stop eating pork because of that?

His eyelids were growing heavy. A young man at the table next to him asked him a question in English, which he didn't understand. Majnun looked around. He had already passed through here, but the buildings didn't seem familiar to him, it was as if he were in a dream and seeing them for the first time. His fingers were swollen, perhaps because of the heat. He thought about Suzana, about Laila. His heart beat rapidly and erratically. He felt like he was suffocating. He had to get out of there fast.

Might Carmen be his savior? If she'd had a cell phone, he would have called her. He certainly wasn't going to call Suzana. The young man at the table next to him again tried to start up a conversation. "I'm sorry," Majnun replied in Portuguese, "I can't understand anything." He called the waiter over, paid his bill, and left, trying to get away from the young man.

He slowly made his way towards the Lavapiés neighborhood, admiring the decadent facades of the buildings. After forty minutes of wandering around, he found a cheap hotel with an internet connection.

He climbed four flights of stairs with his backpack on his shoulders and then lay down, unable to take the Spanish *siesta*. With his eyes glued to the ceiling and his mouth half open, he became submerged in bitter thoughts, debating the various routes his life might take, among which the only clear ones were sickness, death, or prison, unless he traveled to fight somewhere, driven by sorrow, which can sometimes be the author of noble, even heroic, acts.

Time had stopped. It couldn't be measured by units of expectations. Furthermore, when time did pass, it didn't use uniform units of measurement; it wasn't systematic, it surprised one with brutal leaps. Virtue and vice, honor and dishonor, where might they be?

He thought about freeing himself from all scruples in order to experiment with blind sensation, becoming a criminal, without the weight of morality and good reputation, experiencing savage freedom. His heart fluttered when he imagined Suzana's naked body struggling against his on the hotel bed. He should go back to the hotel and confront her, tell her everything. But what could he say? He didn't even know what he wanted, and knew even less about how to be bad. He was even bad at being bad.

Finally, he decided to make an effort to reflect rationally, as if he were another person seeing him, a critic that could observe him from a distance. He thought about the only advice that his grandpa Sérgio had given him, quoting a German philosopher: "Do that which you would want to be converted into universal law." So, as if he had found the path, he took the Arabic Koran out of his backpack. He sat down in a chair, stretched his legs out onto the bed, placed the laptop on his thighs, and got to work. First, he would do research on the internet to understand better the differences between Sunnis and Shiites. Then he would read some *surahs* in his Koran. He soon found some information: after the murder of the fourth caliph, Ali, the first Shiite imam, the caliphate fell into the hands of Muawiya, who had many followers — Sunnis, like his grandma — but he wasn't recognized by the Shiites because, unlike Ali, the cousin and son-in-law of Mohammed, the blood of the prophet did not flow through his veins.

A skullcap does not a Muslim make

It was August 19th, Friday. He woke up early and took a long shower, while going over the previous night's dreams. Carmen and Laila were mixed together in them, and Suzana inexplicably hadn't shown up at all. For the best, he thought. She was insignificant. He never wanted to see her again. Never. Truly, never again! The mere idea of this brought him a shred of joy, which was made visible in the slight smile of the relaxed muscles of his face. He should have slept more, but he was in a good mood. He washed his feet thoroughly, even in between his toes, worried about being embarrassed if they made him wash his feet at the mosque. Friday was a day of celebration, a sanctified day, the Muslim Sunday.

He trimmed his beard and cut his fingernails and toenails in the manner indicated by the bearded American guy. He picked out his best clothes: linen pants, even if they were all wrinkled, and a blue polo shirt. Would his hat function as a substitute for a turban? He put on his dress shoes, instead of the sneakers he'd been walking around in since he'd left Brasilia.

After getting something to eat at Café Barbieri, he studied a map on Google and got on a bus, Koran under his arm, riding towards the mosque on the M-30, the Omar Mosque of Madrid. Forty-five minutes later he arrived at an enormous building, built of the finest marble. Right at the entrance was an anti-terrorism banner. Inside, every door also displayed an anti-terrorist symbol, a black ribbon originally created in opposition to ETA.

After walking through the Islamic Cultural Center, he asked a young woman with a beautiful beige headscarf wrapped around her head that fell in folds halfway down her chest if he could visit the mosque, especially the prayer room. Taking notice of his accent, she directed him to a young man with a long beard and a skullcap on his head, just like the American he'd met in the park, but perhaps a little older than him.

Of Syrian origin, Ahmed had lived in Brazil, just like the Libyan he'd met the night before. But unlike the Libyan, he had learned

Portuguese. He was available to answer any questions Majnun might have.

The arches of the prayer room, he said, were inspired by the Córdoba Mosque. Majnun commented—applying the knowledge he'd gleaned from the internet and speaking as if he'd been to that mosque—that he found it absurd that Christians had built a cathedral inside it, destroying some of the hundreds of marble columns and breaking up the elegant arrangement of the geometric designs of the *azulejo* tiles with ostentatious altars and images of saints. This commentary garnered Ahmed's affection.

Exiting onto one of the courtyards, Majnun noticed the inscription: "There is no God but Allah, and Mohammed is his prophet." In the cafeteria, they drank mint green tea.

"Have you read the Book," asked Ahmed.

"What book?"

"There's only one. The *mushaf.*"

"Ah," said Majnun, the Koran in his hands, "I've read parts."

"When you read the Koran in its entirety, you'll notice that the *surahs* revealed to the Prophet in Mecca correspond to more than two-thirds of the *mushaf,* the Book, and that in the Medina *surahs* there are practical rules for the functioning of society. The year 622, which is the immigration or escape of the Prophet to Medina, is the year of the Hijra, year zero of the Muslim calendar. But it's not enough to just read the Book. You have to understand it. What do you know about Islam?"

"I read that God chose Mohammed to be the messenger of the Koran. And that the binding of the Koran . . ."

"*Mushaf.*"

"Was the task of the first caliph, Abu Bakr, and then of the second caliph, Umar . . ."

"Omar Ibn al Kahttab."

"The third caliph, Uthman, created a commission for the unification of the text and ordered that other versions be destroyed. I also read that there are at least seven different interpretations of the Koran."

"That's a good start. But what do you think Islam is?"

"A religion."

"It's not a religion the way you all define Christian religions."

"I don't define anything, I don't even know if I'm Christian. I've never read the Bible."

"Muslims respect the original Torah and the Gospel of the Prophet Isa or Jesus (peace be upon him), who will return to the Earth near the Final Judgment to restore justice and vanquish the antichrist. But the Koran is the most recent and most perfect of the sacred books. It's the only one with the message of Allah that has been preserved from the beginning, ever since the revelation Allah gave to the Prophet Mohammed through the Angel Jibreel, also known as the Archangel Gabriel."

"But Christians say that Jesus was the son of God, or even God himself."

"No, there is only one Allah. He didn't have a son. On this point, the Koran is clear. Allah is the Arabic word for God. It's not the name of the God of Islam. When I say that Islam isn't a religion the way Christians define religion, I mean that in our theology we don't study God. Islam is the *din*. There is no other god but God, and Mohammed is his messenger. You might imagine that Islam is a profession of faith. But it's not just that. It's submission to Allah, complete renouncement and surrender before God, belief in His will. That's what Islam means. It's also a religion, if you want to use that term, of unification and unity. It unifies all the religions into the religion of God. It unifies the messages of all the prophets. The essence of life and of man is one alone, and that's why we shouldn't distinguish between the material and spiritual parts of our lives, nor between acts of religious ritual and social behaviors, between dogma and law."

He then explained that Islam is the natural religion of humanity. A person is Muslim from the moment they're born. And he quoted a *hadith* of the Prophet: each person is born into the natural religion; it's their parents who make them Christian, Jewish, or Zoroastrian.

"In Islam, the contact between the faithful and God is immediate, direct. The importance given to observed reality, to practical and juridical aspects, leads many people to say that Islam is a religion without mystery, non-dogmatic, exempt from the claims of theological interpretation, and that it doesn't justify itself outside of reason. We don't have sacraments, like Christians. For us, there is no such thing as the Incarnation. There is no Trinity. Nor miracles. And we don't believe that the world was created in six days. Allah is free; no one can force him to do something through magic, that is, through dogmas and sacraments. He is sovereign, pacific, redeeming, powerful ... And do you know why Islam is the religion of the prophets?" asked Ahmed, but he didn't hear a response because he kept on talking without even a pause, not noticing that Majnun had started to make a small movement of his lips.

"The Koran is in the Abrahamic tradition. There are six legislative prophets: Adam, father of all human beings; Noah; Abraham, the friend of God; Moses; Jesus; and, finally, Mohammed. Each of them brought a book containing revelations from God: as you must know, Moses's book is the Torah and Jesus's is the Gospel. The revelation of Islam is the most perfect, because it represents the essence of what came before it. Open your Koran to the third *surah*, verse three."

Majnun looked for it and read: "He has sent down upon you (O Mohammed), the Book in truth, confirming what was before it. And He revealed the Torah and the Gospel."

"As you must know, Jews and Christians are people of the Book, according to the Koran. But Jews and Christians have distorted the original revelations," said Ahmed. "The proof of this is that the Gospel should have been only one. So how did four of them come about?"

Again Majnun made to say something, but wasn't able to interrupt that monologue.

"And there aren't only these six prophets, there were many others, who only brought warnings and predictions, but no books. There have been 124,000 of them."

Majnun thought of Ibrahim and about himself, who might be prophet number 124,001.

"The most important thing for us is the practice of the five pillars: the profession of faith, 'there is no God but God, and Mohammed is his messenger'; prayer five times daily; obligatory charity; fasting at Ramadan; and the pilgrimage to Mecca. Do you know when Ramadan is?"

"I know that it changes every year."

"It's just that it is in the ninth month of the Muslim calendar year, which is lunar, rather than solar. So Ramadan can take place in any season. The lunar year is shorter than the solar year and doesn't correspond to the seasons. Some months have twenty-nine days, others have thirty. And do you know the times of day for prayers?"

"More or less."

"The prayer at dawn takes place between the first light of day and the rising of the sun; the noonday prayer starts when the sun is in the middle of the sky and ends when the shadow of an object becomes the same size as the object; the afternoon prayer starts when the shadow of an object is the same size as the object and ends when the shadow has grown to double the size of the object; the sunset or dusk prayer is done between the setting of the sun and the last light of day; the nighttime prayer, between the last reflected light of the sun and the first hint of the light of the following day."

"And what happens if someone lives at the North Pole?"

"The rules can be reinterpreted."

"What confuses me are the different interpretations that can be made of the Koran."

"If you read it closely, the words of the Book are precise. They cannot be interchanged or modified by synonyms. But the Koran isn't only a text, the *mushaf*. It should be understood in its totality, as a coherent complex of principles and values. Just as it gave answers to the society of Mohammed's time, the response of God through the mind of the Prophet, it can also give answers to our society. So, minor adaptations are necessary and perfectly acceptable."

"But there's so much discord between the different sects . . ."

"Between good Muslims there isn't, nor should there be, any discord, for they know the forty-ninth *surah*, which asserts, in verse ten: 'The believers are brothers, so make settlement between your brothers.'"

As he spoke, Ahmed punctuated his sentences with affirmative

JOÃO ALMINO

gestures of his head and firm movements of his hands, as if his arguments needed those gestures to strengthen their persuasive power.

"It is said in the Koran that Allah taught mankind, through
Adam, all of the names, and introduced them to the angels, ordering
them to bow down before the human creation. All of them bowed,
save Iblis, that is, Lucifer, and that's why he became Satan, the greatest enemy of mankind. The knowledge that men have of the names
revealed by Allah makes them, however, greater than the very angels."

Majnun lowered his eyes, lost in thought. He wasn't sure what he
should say. Finally, he asked:

"But do you believe that Mohammed rose into the heavens on
a winged horse?"

"It's part of our faith."

"If I wanted to convert, how would I do it?"

"Proclaim in all sincerity—three times in the presence of two witnesses—the *Shahada*, the Islamic profession of faith: *Ashadu `anla
ilaha illal-Lah, wa`ashadu `anna muhammadan rasulul-Lah*, which
means, 'I testify that there is no other divinity but God, and that
Mohammed is his prophet.'"

Majnun made a note on a little piece of paper: "a skullcap does
not a Muslim make." Ahmed was nothing like the other bearded
guy, who also wore a skullcap, whom he'd met in Buen Retiro Park.

Still the Egyptian astrologer

It was Saturday, the 20th, when Majnun returned to the guesthouse.

"Shit, where have you been?" asked Carmen. "We looked everywhere. And we contacted the police."

"The police?"

"What did you want us to do? Shit, you disappeared. You could have at least called to tell us you were all right."

"I wasn't all right."

Suzana didn't throw him out of the room, but she also didn't speak a single word to him.

Majnun lowered his head. He didn't have answers to Carmen's questions, not even the simplest of them.

"Tell me one thing. What about your grandparents, what do you think they are thinking, huh?" asked Carmen.

"You contacted my grandparents too?"

"It had been two days, dude. I got your grandpa Dario's phone number from Pablo's dad, whom I'm going to have to call and let him know you're alive. Since no one ever answered the phone, Suzana had to ask her dad to keep trying to reach them. He's the one who gave the news to your grandpa. You really need to call your grandpa yourself."

"It wasn't a full two days."

"We're not going to argue over trivial details."

Carmen called Pablo's dad and then announced that she was going over to his apartment.

"He invited us to go to Granada," she added. "As well as for lunch tomorrow. And asked me to remind you about the conference on Monday."

Suzana left with her. She was going to attend the Church events.

Majnun sat alone in front of his computer. He read about the revelation to Mohammed, beginning in Mecca, where over twelve years he wrote the first *surahs*, preaching love, brotherhood, peace, liberty, and equality, even among men and women. This period of revelation lasted until the Hijra, when the Prophet fled to Medina to escape persecution. In this second period the revelations continued for ten years and produced the Medinan *surahs*, which contain juridical content, with arguments against idolatry and defense against enemies.

Majnun reached the conclusion that Islam was a religion of equality. Everyone made the pilgrimage. Everyone practiced abstinence during Ramadan. And everyone had similar graves in a simple cemetery.

At noon, very early in Brazil, he received a phone call from his grandpa Dario, who angrily ordered him to return immediately. It didn't matter if he went to jail. If he thought he was innocent, he could offer a defense.

He got on the internet. No news about him or the crime he was supposed to have committed. No new emails from Laila, either.

He spent the rest of the afternoon doing research for his novella and for an essay on tolerance in Islam that would appear in the dialogue of the characters and commentary by the narrator. He read about Asturias, where the family of his grandpa Sérgio hailed from. There was information about the region in the era of the Celts, about its conquest by the Romans in the first century BC and by the Visigoths in the fifth century AD. He had a thirst for knowledge. He had to study, to learn.

He didn't want to leave and was going to stay in the room reading. If Muslims could fast throughout all of Ramadan, he could manage to fast for at least a day.

He read about the fall of Granada, the subject that interested him the most and which would be the principal subject of his novella. By the time of the Treaty of Alcalá de Henares in 1308, the kingdoms of Castile and Aragon — with Aragon having the possibility of an alliance with the king of Morocco — had already decided to destroy the kingdom of Granada, in a war upon which Pope Clement V conferred the title of crusade.

He went back to reading about Ibrahim and introduced into the new version of the novella the possibility of Ibrahim receiving Laila in exchange for his defense of the kingdom of Granada. In one of the defense operations, when the troops of Sultan Aben Habuz—directed by the bronze horseman—advanced in the direction of the enemy, they found only a beautiful Christian princess, with whom the sultan fell in love. Protected from his enemies and in the company of the princess, the sultan had only one desire: a tranquil, solitary place where he could take refuge from the world. With the knowledge he had from *The Book of Wisdom*, Ibrahim promised him he would rebuild a famous garden and palace, one of the wonders of Arabia, referenced in the Koran. Because of his pride, arrogance, and presumptuousness, its founder had been punished with the disappearance of that garden and palace, which were then only visible to wanderers in the desert, as it once had been visible to Ibrahim. The sultan promised to give him whatever he desired in exchange for the reconstruction of that earthly paradise. On one of the entrances, a gate in the wall that surrounded the palace, Ibrahim engraved two talismans: a hand and a key. As long as the hand at the top of the gate never fell upon the key below it, that place, situated on a beautiful hill, would be protected.

In exchange for this, Ibrahim only requested that when the first saddled horse passed through the gate with the talismans, he be rewarded with the load that the horse was carrying, to which the sultan agreed. The construction work concluded, he informed the sultan that he would only be able to see it once he had passed through the gate for the first time.

On the appointed day, Ibrahim and the sultan were walking side by side, with the princess in front of them, mounted atop a white saddled horse. When she passed through the gate, Ibrahim demanded his reward, disappeared with the princess into a chasm he split open in the hill, and closed it up after him, leaving no trace. And the two of them would remain in that sumptuous subterranean palace forever, or at least until the hand would fall upon the key, undoing the magic of the enchanted hill.

The two of them: he, Majnun, and Laila. Yes, the legend had to be modified, it was his story now, and the princess of his story would be Laila, who would become his wife. But in that era a wife was just the first among many of the husband's women. To reduce her workload, give her more amusement, and enable her to bear more easily the weight of having a husband, she would prefer to have other women around. Why not another Christian slave, transformed into his concubine? Suzana. Suzana was Catholic, even very Catholic, though she was the daughter of a Jew.

"I'm Catholic, but not an idiot," Suzana had once said, wearing a tiny yellow bikini at the poolside, when, surrounded by friends, one of them assumed that since she was very Catholic, she must agree with the Church's most conservative positions on divorce, sex outside of marriage, abortion, and gay marriage.

He, Majnun, was going to get lost in all those stories, unless, as in the *Thousand and One Nights*, he made good use of all of them, his novella consisting of one story inside another story inside another story, on top of the essay, which would traverse all of those stories.

"Shit, you're always on your computer," said Carmen when she got back. "You like machines more than people."

"I was reading about zero," said Majnun. "Did you know that Arabs introduced the concept of zero to Europe? Nothing times a million is still nothing, zero times a million is zero, of course, no doubt about it. But how do you explain that the million that already exists suddenly disappears when it's multiplied by zero? Zero has this ability to make existing things disappear. So zero isn't the same thing as nothing. It's magic. Pure magic. Don't you think?"

"You should have a chat with Pablo's dad, he's a specialist on the Arab occupation of the Iberian Peninsula."

He had received numbers of invitations during his internet wanderings. He could join groups in Afghanistan, Syria, Lebanon, Egypt . . . His browser was open to a Moroccan site.

"Be careful with your internet searches! These days everything is monitored. The Americans and the British know every last keystroke of what you're searching. And they'll put you on a list of suspects. They'll say you've come from the three borders region, which they consider shady, and then, brother, you're screwed."

Majnun was interested to know whether, after conversion and in order to be a good Muslim, he would have to take part in jihad against the infidels. Would Professor Rodrigo Díaz's conference on Monday clear this up for him?

He had read many verses from the Koran: one said that, in confrontations with infidels, dialogue and persuasion should prevail; in another, that it was necessary to combat those who don't believe in God or the Final Judgment Day, as well as those who don't abstain from that which God and His Messenger have forbidden; a third one commanded them to kill idolaters, yet opening the path to salvation for them if they repented and observed the hours of prayer. Some thought that this last verse abrogated the 124 verses that come before it. Others felt that the second part of it was self-abrogating.

Were there twenty abrogated verses in the Koran? Forty-two? Or as many as 240?

The West does not exist

On Sunday, Carmen and Majnun went on foot through the old city of Madrid to join the professor for the lunch he'd invited them to. They hadn't dressed in Brazilian colors on purpose, though she was in a yellow dress, and he in a blue cap and green T-shirt. They passed through the Puerta del Sol, continued on towards the Plaza Mayor, walked down Calle Mayor to the Palacio Real, and arrived at a wide avenue. Divorced, Pablo's father lived alone in a large apartment on the Paseo del Pintor Rosales.

The professor, impeccably clean-shaven, wearing a blue long-sleeved shirt and well-pressed brown linen pants, welcomed Carmen with a kiss on either cheek and gave Majnun a hug. Suzana and Pablo were already at the apartment, sitting on one of the sofas in the living room, Pablo holding her hand. Desire appeared to have constructed a bridge between atheism and religiosity. The white of the sofa accentuated Pablo's black shirt and Suzana's blue dress with white polka dots, which only fell halfway down her thighs.

She tugged at the hem of her dress, as if it were elastic, protecting herself from Majnun's stare. Majnun tried to forget the scenes from that night with her, but the images were insistent, like the projection of a film that won't stop winding around the reels as he continued to see even though he'd closed his eyes.

The books on the dark wooden shelves that covered two entire walls continued down the hallway.

"Four thousand volumes," the professor informed them.

In a room that was contiguous to the living room and visible from it, wooden filing cabinets were brimming with documents.

"I need to organize all that material," he continued.

Assuming they were all students, the professor wanted to know what they were studying, forgetting the response that Majnun had given him when he'd visited Brasilia. Carmen said that she wanted to work, not study. Suzana, that she studied economics.

Majnun reminded him that he had failed the entrance exams for history.

"I'm a '*nini*,' as you say around here, a neither-nor. I'm neither in school nor working. My utopia would be to become a '*mileurista*,' as you also say around here, earn a thousand euros a month."

"And Carmen tells me that you're a descendant of Spaniards?"

"On my paternal grandfather's side, the one you don't know, who lives in São Paulo. My family is from Asturias."

"A place that's full of history. The Moors, when they arrived on the Iberian Peninsula, were unable to conquer the region. It was a refuge for noble Christians, who founded the first Christian kingdom."

"Spain is a country of ghosts. Christian ghosts. Muslim ghosts," said Majnun.

"Opus Dei is not a ghost," said Pablo in disagreement.

"I was reading about the expulsion of the Jews," said Majnun.

"Unjust treatment of a people that came to this peninsula back in the era of Emperor Hadrian in the second century," said the professor.

"True. I read that when the Arabs got here, there were already Jews," replied Majnun.

"Of course. They had been persecuted by the Visigoths. Because of that they welcomed the Arab invasions of Spain with open arms. You all have to visit Granada. You can stay at our house, in the Albayzín district. Well, by then, they were already well established in Albayzín, as well as the hill in front of it, to such an extent that the Arabs called that place Granada of the Jews. Would you like some red wine?" he asked, opening a bottle. "According to a well-known historical text from the fourteenth century, *Historia de los Reyes de la Alhambra*, written in exile by the Granadino vizier Lisan ad-Din ibn al-Khatib, in most ways it looked like Syria. Its wide *vega* was compared to the Ghuta, the valley or *vega* of Damascus."

In the presence of the professor's erudition, Majnun felt like a despicable rat. Could he someday become a respectable intellectual like him? As knowledgeable as him? No, never. If he hadn't even been able to pass the entrance exams . . .

"How is your research on tolerance in Islam going?" asked the professor.

Majnun's face couldn't hide his joy: the professor really had remembered the conversation they'd had in Brasilia!

"It's stupid to talk about tolerance in Islam," said Suzana, interrupting them, furious. "There are places where blasphemy and apostasy are punished by death; where women can't drive or ride a bike. They have to be accompanied by a male relative in order to leave the house, even if it's just a child. They need their husband's permission to travel . . ."

"That has nothing to do with the religion . . . In Tunis, Cairo, Istanbul you'll find liberated Muslim women who don't wear the headscarf, feminists," argued Majnun.

"Have you ever been there?"

"No, but . . ."

"And why are the majority of terrorists Muslim? Do you think it's because they're unable to read the Koran correctly? Or do they read it and blow themselves up with bombs, thinking that martyrs go to the Garden of Delights, full of virgins with large, black eyes?"

"Sometimes what is at play in the Arab world is ethnic or religious rivalry, especially between Sunnis and Shiites," said Rodrigo.

"Christians also fought amongst themselves. And look, to this day Protestants and Catholics don't get along in Northern Ireland," said Pablo.

"That's not relevant to this discussion," continued Rodrigo. "Egypt and Morocco are countries with a grand historical tradition. But other Arab countries owe their creation to European colonialism. In many of them, the weakening of the dictatorship strengthens religious and tribal rivalries, which favors the radicals."

Suzana tugged her dress down over her thighs again and asserted:

"They have modern techniques and weapons of war, but their mentality is medieval. They don't think at all about the future. They're reactionaries who want to take us back to the Middle Ages."

"That's what I want too," said Majnun.

"Don't even joke about it," retorted Suzana.

The professor poured several glasses of wine.

"The wine's from Toro," he said, then turned to Suzana. "You have a point, that's the thinking of the fundamentalists, who feel that the past, especially the time of the Prophet and the early caliphs, was perfect. The great examples are Abu Bakr, the first caliph, who created the foundations of the State, and Umar, the second caliph, who created the foundations of the empire by initiating the conquest of lands outside of Arabia, like Syria, Palestine, Iraq, and Egypt. A golden age, as they see it, which needs to be brought back. An anti-utopian idea. The thing is, that 'golden age' was a troubled one. Suffice it to say that Uthman, the third caliph, was assassinated and the next one, Ali, the first Shiite imam, was also assassinated, after a tumultuous five-year reign. There's no doubt that many radicals want, in this day and age, to create an Islamic state that can defend itself against what they see as an atheistic, corrupt Western society."

"It's a consequence . . ." Majnun wanted to develop a line of thought, but Rodrigo interrupted him:

"It's just that this isn't anything new. Do you know what the religious fundamentalists of the nineteenth century thought? That abolishing slavery in Tunisia was against Islam and was only done in order to appease the West. For isn't slavery part of Sharia? Of course it is. It's a logical problem for present-day fundamentalists: if they accept that slavery no longer makes sense, they have to admit that the Islamic law is a human creation and must evolve like other bodies of law. If they should abandon slavery, why not corporal punishment, polygamy, or discrimination against women? If they considered it a divine, immutable law, then they couldn't abolish slavery."

"What I find most interesting about Spain is the Arabic influence," asserted Majnun. "Even Madrid itself is a city of Arabic origin, isn't it?"

"Why are you so obsessed with the Moors?" asked Suzana, still livid, feeling hurt because of something only she and Majnun knew about.

"Artichoke, which you love so much, is an Arabic word," said Majnun.

"So is assassin," replied Suzana drily.

Despite the querulous tone of voice of someone who wanted to contradict him and perhaps accuse him, Majnun was pleased that Suzana was at least addressing him.

"What happened to that great civilization you all are talking about? It has nothing to do with the present day. What happened to all the mathematicians, geographers, doctors, astronomers, architects? They remained in the Middle Ages. Since that time, what have the Arabs contributed to civilization, to art, to science? And, above all, to peace? There are crazy fundamentalists out there who are even against music and cinema. In Iran they invented an electric machine for cutting off the hands of a thief, and flagellation is a common punishment: seventy-four lashes for a woman who appears in a public place without a headscarf. Do you, Sir, think there is a clash of civilizations?" asked Suzana as she turned to the professor, gesticulating angrily with a wine glass in her hand and spilling a drop of red wine on her dress with the white polka dots.

"First of all, Iran isn't Arabic. Secondly, there is an explanation for those corporal punishments. Modern penal laws exist in order to rehabilitate the prisoner or ensure that he doesn't commit the crime again once he is released. Now, ancient penal laws, which still predominate in Sharia law, have the objective of making one suffer. You need to understand the following: the modern penal code relies on the existence of the State, prisons, and the police. Where these things didn't exist, the solution was corporal punishment. The law of retaliation (eye for an eye, tooth for a tooth) was present in Hammurabi's Code as well as the Hebrew Bible. It was an improvement when, under Sharia law, corporal punishments stopped being meted out by the families of the victims and no longer degenerated into tribal wars. Of course in this day and age, I agree with you," said Rodrigo, turning to Suzana, "that they no longer make sense. But we have to admit that Islamic law was a legal advancement in its time," continued the professor in his nasal voice. "In ancient Greece, a foreigner wasn't protected by the laws of the city, couldn't defend his rights in court, couldn't even marry or buy property. Throughout all of antiquity, even under Roman Law, prisoners of war were always enslaved. Mosaic law allowed polygamy and restricted inheritance to male heirs. In medieval Europe, the law of primogeniture prevailed, reserved only for male progeny. Compared with these legal systems, Islamic law marks an improvement when it came to foreigners and non-Muslims, slaves, and women."

"It's possible to say that there was tolerance in . . ." Majnun started to explain, but Rodrigo ignored him and continued his line of reasoning:

"It recommended that slaves be treated properly and insinuated that it would be more convenient to free them, limited polygamy to four wives and recommended monogamy at a time when there were no limits to polygamy. Considering a woman as an heir, for example, even if they only received half of what men did, went further than European laws, which didn't recognize inheritance for women. What happened was that, while other laws continued to evolve, Islamic law stagnated because of rigid interpretations about its divine origin. Finally, and I say this with full conviction, there are no more civilizations. There is only one, which is continuously modified by contributions from various places. The West doesn't exist. Neither does the East."

"What do you mean they don't exist?" Suzana interjected brusquely, irritated.

"They used to exist, of course," continued the professor with no change in tone of voice. "But even when they did exist, it was a mixture. They were always changing, always in motion. Look at Europe, which is considered the center of Western civilization. It was constantly receiving outside influence, from the Arabs, the Chinese . . . like the olive tree—mentioned in a *surah* entitled 'The Light' in the Koran—it is neither Eastern nor Western . . . Civilization is a process that is ever unfinished, receiving influences from the most diverse sources; in our day, above all, influences from the technological and scientific revolutions and the revolution of information. The four cardinal directions don't divide the world; instead it's weakness and power, ignorance and knowledge, justice and injustice, tyranny and liberty."

"But there are Christian countries and Islamic countries," insisted Suzana.

"Those don't exist either," replied the professor, with his customary calmness. "There are secular countries, where one can profess whatever religion one chooses, and countries with an official religion, some of which are more or less tolerant of other creeds. Personally, I don't think that the future is in identifying roots, figuring out whom a determined territory first belonged to, and turning a nation, a tribe, or a religion into the legitimate heirs of their ancestors. The future is in accepting the multiple identities that will continue to take different forms, as well as transcultural mixtures. Deep down, we're all foreigners, strangers to our lands. There is a beautiful *hadith* from the Prophet Mohammed that says: 'Islam was born as something strange, it will end as it began, strange; blessed are the strangers.'"

"I would like to have lived in Granada during the height of its golden age," said Majnun.

"How horrible," protested Suzana, trying to wipe the drop of wine off her dress with her finger.

"Why horrible? There was more tolerance in Granada than in the Christian kingdoms," said Majnun.

"You deserve to have lived there and died of the plague," she replied.

"The best thing to do is pour a little white wine, then put some fine salt on it, then rinse with water," Pablo told Suzana. Then he disappeared down the hallway with Suzana, who walked like a heron in her white high-heeled shoes, which matched her handbag and left the red polish on her toenails almost entirely exposed.

"Rodrigo surely knows this subject better than you," said Carmen, calling the professor by his first name.

Suzana returned with Pablo, who brought back bottles of water and white wine. Suzana was carrying the salt shaker.

"Actually, the period I would like to go back to and live through is the apex of the culture of Granada. Which was during the reign of Yusuf I, wasn't it, professor?" asked Majnun.

"I see you've been reading about the history of the Arab

occupation," replied Rodrigo. "Yusuf I came to power in 1333 and was assassinated in 1354. Another period of glory was the reign of Mohammed V."

"*Venga*, despite that assassination, do you still want to go to Granada with us?" Pablo asked Majnun.

"He's reading about it for a novel he's writing, right, Majnun?" said Carmen.

"A novella," he clarified.

"Of course, *vale, vale, vale*," said Pablo, repeating the word "*vale*" with the speed of an automaton.

The professor went off with Carmen to the room filled with file cabinets. They disappeared from view.

"And what if Boabdil hadn't had such bad luck and had defeated the Catholic monarchs?" asked Majnun.

"Dude, you're obsessed with this," said Suzana.

"It's like my dad always says: unfortunately there are no 'what ifs' in history. What if Phillip II's armada, which was considered invincible, hadn't been destroyed by a hurricane and had managed to disembark its twenty thousand soldiers in England in 1588? There would be no Protestant England, and the balance of powers in Europe would be different," argued Pablo. "Furthermore: the conquest of Granada wasn't an isolated action of Fernando and Isabel. The occupation had been announced in the thirteenth century. Granada only maintained its independence by paying taxes. So, even in that golden age in which you'd like to live, Granada was already dependent on Castile."

"But it would've been great to live in that era, because the Muslims were generous, magnanimous . . ." Majnun began to argue, before being interrupted by the Spaniard:

"Cruel. Don't forget this: Islam celebrated the concept of jihad, holy war. Jihad was no slouch compared to the crusades and the military orders of Calatrava, Santiago, and Alcántara."

"But we need to undo the false impression that the expansion of Islam was achieved by wars of conquest. In Central and West Africa and Southeast Asia, where the majority of Muslims live, it expanded peacefully," said the professor as he returned to the living room, a book in his hand and accompanied by Carmen.

"No, don't interrupt me, we were talking about the Iberian Peninsula," said Pablo. "And I'll ask you something: where would democracy be? Because democracy was introduced by the Christians."

"Actually, it would have been better for the advancement of democracy if the monarchs of Aragon and Castile hadn't won the war against the Moors once and for all, if there had still been people inhabiting the borderlands, fighting for their freedom. Personal liberties and freedom of movement came about in cities which, on strips of land that separated the Christians and the Moors, acquired powers that were independent of the Christian kingdoms, developed self-governance, created their own laws and jurisdictions, as well as assemblies in which direct democracy was practiced. Well then: those liberties came to an end when the Catholic monarchs won the war against Islam. Isabel and Fernando sacrificed the civil authority of those cities. The unification of the monarchy brought about authoritarian, absolute power, the Counter-Reformation, censorship, and the Inquisition."

"Exactly," said Majnun, pleased at the support he was receiving from the professor. "The Catholic conquest, and the accompanying expulsion of the Jews and Muslims, put an end to cultural hybridism."

"Hybridism isn't enough. It's necessary to impose an idea," argued Suzana. "And Christianity won out."

"*Venga*, that tolerant, multicultural, Islamic Spain never existed. And you know that better than anybody," said Pablo in disagreement, addressing his father. "Is that your book? Give it to Majnun, so he can read about the massacres of the Jews."

"At that time it wasn't a crime to kill in the name of Christ or Santiago," argued Suzana.

Carmen thought that it didn't matter at all who won this war or that one, women would always be discriminated against, as they still are, especially in the Arab world.

"But Saudi Arabia and Tunisia aren't the same thing. Which

proves that it isn't a problem of ethnicity or religion," argued Majnun.

The professor stood watching the debate with a book in his hand and a grin of superiority in his lips.

"Perhaps this little book will be of interest to you," he said to Majnun.

Majnun leafed through its pages.

"I want a dedication."

From the azulejo tiles printed on the cover of the book, the discussion turned to Islam, and from there to present-day Tunisia and Egypt, where the Tamarod — "revolt" in Arabic — youth movement had not yet come into existence, and neither had the military regime returned. We were still in 2011, and the Arab Spring signified hope. Finally, the subject turned to the lecture that the professor was going to give the following day.

"I'll be there," said Majnun.

"Rodrigo has invited me to work with him," said Carmen as they went back to the *hostal*.

"Doing what?" asked Majnun.

"Organizing his papers. Didn't you see the mess? And he can put me up for free."

"You're going to stay in Spain?"

"I'm not sure yet."

"But your visa is going to expire."

"I don't even care about that. They aren't going to keep me from leaving. And once I leave, I don't intend to come back."

The next day, Monday, Majnun attended professor Rodrigo's lecture. In a spacious room at Complutense University, he explained the references to jihad in the Koran, a topic in which Majnun had become greatly interested ever since he'd begun to frequent certain websites. According to him, the word "jihad" appeared only four times in the Koran, and it couldn't be confirmed that it precisely signified "holy war."

Majnun, sitting in one of the front rows, was probably the most attentive listener of anyone in the audience. He tried not to miss a single word and he wrote down everything he could on his laptop.

"The first time the word 'jihad' appears is in the twenty-second *surah*, verse seventy-eight, which talks about undertaking jihad with boldness in the way of Allah," the professor asserted in his nasal voice.

Then he cited another passage that talks of jihad in the way of Allah being above attachment to family, tribe, or material goods.

"Many argue," he said, standing behind a desk and drinking water to clear his throat, "that this is in reference to spiritual rather than military combat. The translation 'holy war' is even less applicable to the mention of jihad as a way to combat those who are incredulous of the Koran. One reference that might be closer to 'armed conflict' is the one that commands the faithful—when leaving to fight jihad for the cause of Allah—not to take the enemy as a confidant, not to trust them with their private matters.

"But jihad," the professor continued, "could be better translated as force, commitment, which could be military or merely moral. According to an important theological interpretation, the major jihad would be a fight for self-purification, to combat proclivities of character and behavior, while the minor jihad would correspond to war.

"When the Koran clearly refers to armed combat," proceeded the professor, "it uses '*qatala*,' which means 'war,' a word that is present already in the second *surah*."

He then put on his glasses, opened the copy of the Koran he had on the desk, and spoke:

"Verse 190 of this *surah* reads as follows: 'Fight in the way of Allah those who fight you, but do not transgress. Indeed, because Allah does not like transgressors.' And verse 191 adds: "And kill them wherever you overtake them and expel them from wherever they have expelled you, and persecution is worse than killing. And do not fight them at the Sacred Mosque unless they fight you there. But if they fight you, then kill them."

It was true that at times the *mujahideen*, those who undertook jihad, concluded the professor, were those who fought in a military sense.

"The Koran affirms: Not equal are those believers remaining at home—other than the disabled—and the *mujahideen*, who strive and fight in the cause of Allah with their wealth and their lives. But they should also impose limits on combat: say to those who have disbelieved that if they cease, what has previously occurred will be forgiven of them."

He went on to make a few other points, which Majnun found less interesting. The discussion as a whole seemed quite inconclusive to him. He only didn't leave before it was over so as not to be disrespectful or rude. After all, the professor had been generous in letting them use his house in Granada.

He would accompany his friends to Granada, but still had to decide what to do after that: whether he would travel to Africa or the Middle East.

Not even heaven is perfect

It was August 23rd, Thursday. The Pope had already left and the World Youth Day had come to a close. Carmen, Suzana, Majnun, and Pablo were on a train, occupying two bench seats, one facing the other, on a four-and-a-half-hour trip. Suzana asked to trade places with Pablo. It gave her motion sickness to travel facing away from the direction of the train. Majnun, next to the window, was staring as if he were lost in thought and seemed not to even hear the friends around him. Noticing his absentmindedness, Carmen waved her hand in front of his eyes:

"Wake up, Majnun," she softly whispered in his ear.

"Where are we?"

"I heard that your grandpa is very worried about you."

"Yeah. Why?"

"Look, you know. You can tell me anything. I'll always be on your side," she continued to whisper in his ear.

"I don't have anything to tell you."

And then he added, for all to hear:

"When we get to Granada, I want to make an expedition to the peak of Mulhacén, in the Sierra Nevada, where Boabdil's father buried his treasure. The Moors left behind lots of buried treasures. When they had to abandon their lands, they thought it would only be for a short while and they'd soon return."

In Granada, they stayed at the house in Albayzín that Rodrigo had recently inherited from his deceased mother. It was on a street that came up from the Carrera del Darro, with a view of the hills of the Alhambra. It was empty, and a fine layer of dust had accumulated on the few pieces of furniture.

That night, Majnun received an email from his grandma Elvira with the news that his grandpa had been hospitalized and was in serious condition. Heart problems. Had he caused his grandpa's illness? He'd left home, traveled abroad without telling him, the police were on his trail, he'd disappeared for two days, ignored his grandpa's orders to come home . . . He had been cruel to him.

"I'm truly despicable, a piece of shit," he said aloud to himself.

Carmen went out with him to a bar near the Plaza de Santa Ana. He wouldn't stop drinking.

"I have to go back to Brasilia. Now, just like my grandpa told me to. Do you think there's still a flight from here to Madrid tonight? Or a bus?"

"Make your decision calmly," she advised. "Drinking doesn't solve anything. At any rate, the train only leaves in the afternoon. We're going to the Alhambra early tomorrow morning. If we're in line by seven thirty in the morning, I've been told that we're guaranteed to get in. And think about it: it might not make a difference if you rush back to see your grandpa."

Carmen observed the sad look on his face and tried to guess what was going through his mind. She kissed him tenderly on the cheek.

"You can tell me. I'll understand. And I'll always be on your side, like I said. Trust me."

"Tell you what?"

"I know. Everyone knows. Didn't you kill Laila's husband?"

"I don't know."

"How can you not know?"

"It's true, I don't know. The police are the ones that say they know. And they must have figured out the IP address of my computer. They can find me easily enough."

He had read a *hadith* of the Prophet that says that "actions are judged by intentions." While the act itself—that is, the murder—was in doubt, there was no doubt about his intention.

On the walk back—along the Carrera del Darro on the banks of the Darro River, which separates, with the constant and tranquil sound of running water, the Albayzín from the forest and hill of the Alhambra, and above which two small bridges span the distance—Carmen told him that she had finally decided to stay for a while in Madrid. She was going to accept Pablo's dad's invitation to work and live in his apartment.

"You can't be serious. You're going to live with that old guy?"

"Just for a few months. There's nothing wrong with that. And what about you? You're in love with a much older woman."

"Older than me, but still young."

They walked with sorrowful steps, which became even more sorrowful when, at the bus stop for the number thirty-one bus, Majnun spotted a sign for the "Paseo de los Tristes," "promenade of the sorrowful." When they arrived back at the house, he pulled from his backpack the deck of cards that he'd bought off the old Belgian in the Garden of Salvation:

"Look here," he said to Carmen. "'In the beginning was desire, the seed of thought.'"

"That must be for you. Not me."

"Do you agree that 'in men, desire begets love; and in women love begets desire'? That's not on one of the cards. It's a quote from Swift."

"Swift? Sounds like a brand of meat."

That night Majnun had trouble sleeping. In his light sleep, near dawn, he dreamed that he was staying in the beachfront house of some old friends. They heard a loud boom. His friends, including Laila, started running towards the sea. He intuited that, in order to protect himself, he should run in the opposite direction and get to a white building that was a few stories high. He knew that he could take refuge in a small studio on the top floor. Through the window he saw, coming from the sky above the sea, an enormous North Korean missile with a nuclear warhead attached. A wave arose from the sea and swept over the land. Would his friends be able to save themselves? He looked: the house had been completely destroyed. His friends, however, had survived and were walking in his direction, Laila in front of the others. He went down to meet them and felt the obligation to put them all up in his studio, though it would be tight quarters. Laila complained that he had abandoned them. She was right. He was a coward and a traitor, but he covered it up: he had gone in the opposite direction to find a place where they could all be safe.

Why those images of destruction? Why North Koreans in a dream in Granada? Why nuclear weapons?

It was not yet seven in the morning, and they were walking over to the Alhambra, the "crimson castle." In the line to buy tickets, Majnun, with dark circles under his eyes, complained to Carmen that he had hardly slept from thinking about his grandpa.

Carmen tenderly rubbed him on the back. During the two-hour wait, she at times put her arm around him and squeezed his hands, reading her friend's mental state in his face. He was wearing — over chest and stomach — the small backpack he'd received at World Youth Day, which he'd taken out of his larger backpack early in the morning. He'd swapped out the Gospels and the catechism for his iPad and a bottle of water.

Finally, they entered and joined a tour group. A guide was giving explanations about the founder of the Alhambra in a continental Portuguese accent:

"Ibn Al Ahmar or Mohammed I, in the year 635 of the Hijri calendar or 1238 of the Gregorian calendar. Because of his ruddy face and the color of his beard, the Moors called him Al Ahmar, 'the red.' And because the Moors called him that, he chose a vivid red for his insignias. And the later kings of Granada followed suit."

They left the guide and took a path heading towards the Palacio de Generalife, observing the landscape, quiet and perfect despite the tourists. The Koran was right: paradise was a garden traversed by a river.

They passed in front of the Gate of Wells, *Bab Al Ghudour* in Arabic, now called the Tower of the Seven Floors, the gate through which Boabdil left Granada for the last time, delivering the palace into the hands of the Catholic monarchs, with the condition that no one else ever enter through that gate. The gate was closed and could only be seen from afar, on the path that led from the Alhambra to the gardens of Generalife — *Jannat Al Arif*, the garden of the architect.

"There are ghosts of Moors here," said Majnun.

"Of course there are," replied Pablo, ironically.

After visiting Generalife, they wandered over to the Gate of Justice, on the arches of which they saw an open hand and a key.

There they listened to the explanation of a different tour guide, in Spanish this time:

"The five fingers signify the five pillars of the Islamic creed, the profession of faith, prayer, charity, fasting, and the pilgrimage. The key is a symbol of faith or power. It is the key of David, transmitted to the Prophet Mohammed. One legend says that when the hand falls and touches the key, all of the buildings of the Alhambra will be destroyed and the treasures buried beneath the gate by the Moors will be uncovered, but this could also be the end of the world."

They entered the Nasrid palaces, admiring each room, astonished at the rich, refined geometrical designs, free of paintings and representations of human figures.

They arrived at the Courtyard of the Myrtles, also known as the Courtyard of the Pool, rectangular and surrounded by shrubs and flowers. The perfect reflecting pool showed the buildings alongside it, the arcades beyond, and the flat sky, an intense blue. Majnun had the strange feeling that he was going to be imprisoned in the Tower of Comares that was reflected in the pool, where Boabdil and his mother were imprisoned.

"Alberca, *al-birka*, from the Arabic word for well or fountain," said Majnun, eager to show off the facts he knew.

For a few seconds he saw his grandpa reflected in the water. No, it couldn't be. He looked all around him. A woman passed by in a *niqab*, carrying a child wearing a Barcelona jersey. He followed her until he became fixated on another woman—pale skinned, her face withered, embittered, and pathetic—who was strolling through the garden. She had a tragic look about her and was dressed all in black. She walked back and forth, back and forth. Moving her arms as if ceaselessly rowing. Her dark eyes, surrounded by dark circles that looked as if they'd been painted with charcoal, scanned the walls. The woman, her forehead covered in wrinkles, darkened the resplendent sun and the blueness of the morning.

"Don't stare at people like that," Carmen advised him, finding Majnun's behavior abnormal, especially when, in the Hall of Ambassadors, he remained out on the veranda of the central window for a long time.

He was thinking about Boabdil's surrender, his departure from Granada to a fiefdom in the Alpujarra Mountains, taking with him all that he wished, which is to say hundreds of horses carrying families, belongings, and the disinterred corpses of his ancestors, whom he preferred not to leave in the hands of the enemy. Majnun commented, with an air of melancholy:

"Here in this hall, Boabdil gathered all of his advisors and a delegation of noblemen from the city so they could weigh in on what was to be done. He listened to all of them, including his vizier, Al-Mulih, and then announced the surrender of Granada. It was later found out that this vizier, who negotiated the terms of surrender with the Christians, was also negotiating in his own best interest: he received a lot of money and huge tracts of land."

They continued on to the Courtyard of the Lions, which was under repair. Since 1370, in the splendor of the Nasrid sultanate of Mohammed V, the fountain had been there, sculpted from a single piece of stone, its dodecagonal basin supported by twelve lions, "a lover whose eyelids are brimming with tears," as the verses of Ibn Zamrak say on its outer surface. Three cats were walking around the patio, one white and two covered in white and light yellow patches. Majnun admired the fountain, the arcades, and the walls: open books that wrote their own stories, poems, and phrases from the Koran.

"*Azulejo* tiles were also introduced to the Iberian Peninsula by the Arabs," he recalled.

One of the cats came over to him. More precisely, a female cat, who looked up at him as if she knew him. Majnun had a feeling that he knew her too. More precisely, he did know her. There was a woman inside of her. He was certain of it because those green eyes, venomously seductive, were Laila's eyes. He felt a profound fear, which only failed to paralyze him because it was a precondition of his courage. He boldly stepped towards the cat, which didn't flinch. He gently ran his fingers under her chin. She liked the caress and purred, with amorous eyes that seemed to want to tell him something.

"Speak, Laila!" ordered Majnun. "Can you all hear those noises?" he said, frightened, abruptly turning towards his friends and covering his ears with his hands.

He could hear the murmur of a multitude coming from underneath the courtyard, the vague sounds of chains beneath the lions. He rubbed his hands together; they were slightly shaking.

"Can't you all hear that?" he repeated, still rubbing his hands together. "It's the spirits of the dead Abencerrages."

Pablo laughed.

"No, this isn't a joke. He has mediumistic powers, I've witnessed them. He really could be hearing spirits," said Carmen.

On one side of the courtyard, a door opened onto the Hall of the Abencerrages, a square enclosure, its high cupola decorated with a beautiful rosette in the shape of a star and trellis windows at its base, the ceiling painted gold, red, brown, and blue, the hall where the Abencerrages had been massacred by Boabdil's father.

"Streaks of blood," said Majnun, pointing to the side of the fountain.

He saw blood running down small grooves, like winding veins along the ground. Brought to that fountain one by one, the Abencerrages had been decapitated.

"Stop it," said Carmen.

Majnun looked at Carmen as if he were seeing her for the first time.

"I want to go back to the Courtyard of the Myrtles, to the pool, just to clear something up," he said, thinking about the reflection he'd seen in the water, the anguished face of his grandfather.

When they got to the Courtyard of the Myrtles, he lay down on the ground, facing the pool. He rested his head on his backpack, gently rocking it to accompany the shimmering movements of the reflecting pool. There was life on the other side of it, deep down below, inside the reflected reality. Perhaps even a better life. A form appeared to him deep down in the pool. He was certain now. It was, in fact, his grandfather, already dead, his eyes frightened, his mouth wide open.

He was overcome with a strong desire to plunge into the water. The intense heat impelled him. And it wasn't just the heat. He needed to escape, escape the police, escape to another world. The reflecting pool confused him, made him dizzy and nauseated, and also attracted him like a magnet.

He quickly stood up, overpowering with difficulty the force that pulled him towards the ground. Dizzy and hypnotized, he watched the water, which trembled under the sun. Suddenly, his vision grew dark and, as if struck by a bullet, he fell into the water with all the weight of his body. He felt his head hit the bottom of the pool, where he would remain forever. He no longer needed to return to the surface, the surface of an intolerable reality. He was going to meet up with his grandpa and ask his forgiveness.

Carmen jumped into the water after him. Seeing this, the other two friends jumped in as well.

With his head underwater and already out of breath, Majnun tried to find the bottom of the pool, but his body was being pushed towards the surface, little by little. I'll be dead when I float on the surface, he thought in a fraction of a second.

He was helped along by strong arms—he didn't know whose—which lifted his body onto the edge of the pool. He felt terribly exhausted, almost unable to move his arms and legs. With eyes closed, he felt the light of the sun on his face. He could see red and yellow streaks.

People around him gesticulated and said incomprehensible things. Who were they? And where was he? Certainly in an unknown, mysterious place, perhaps the sum of all places, the place between places, an impossible place.

"The im-pos-si-ble is ne-ces-sa-ry," he managed to stammer out.

The impossible was the most permanent thing in existence, an intangible beacon that indicated the direction to be taken.

He sat up, with much effort. He looked around him. He was completely wet. He saw everything as if it were in an Impressionist painting, the same one he'd seen in Madrid, *Charing Cross Bridge*. The cloudy images were on the verge of disappearing.

Who was that woman in front of him with the worried look?

"Do you belong to some African tribe?" he asked.

"Stop it, Majnun!" shouted Carmen, offended and at the same time hoping to rouse him.

His head was bleeding.

"Are there any medical services here?" asked Carmen.

She and the other two friends, all of them wet, were also sitting facing the sun, attracting the attention of passersby.

"The infirmary is located on the other side of the Palacio de Carlos V," Pablo informed them.

Majnun still had a confused look to him, languidly turning his head in every direction, as if searching for something. That person, who could he be? And that other woman, the one squeezing his arms?

"An accident can be a zero. Time is compressed so that the future, past, and present all fit into a single point, that of the accident," he said.

He was under the impression that no one could see him, but he could see the rest of the world from where he was hidden behind a wooden latticework window. He could perceive all eras at once, like in the Aleph or the delirium of Brás Cubas. Waiting for the Final Judgment, living together in limbo were those who had arrived in the first years after the creation of the world, impatient with the long wait, as well as the recently-arrived, and even the ones who would have the privilege of not having to wait, having attained limbo on the eve of the Final Judgment. An unjust system.

He lived in a single, circular time, without history and, as such, without progress. He thought: reap the present moment and distrust the future; the moment, an abyss slashed open at the point of intersection between two time periods.

"He's delirious," said Pablo, as he picked up Majnun.

"A bout of amnesia," commented Suzana.

Majnun had a vague recollection of the future, as if he had lived in some other time period, in a distant country. He recognized the building. He was at the Alhambra. But what century was it? What year? He had returned to a past in which he'd never lived, to a zero point at a new altitude on the spiral of history.

"Could we be in the year 891 of the Hijra, which corresponds to 1486 of the Gregorian calendar?" he asked with mathematical precision and after much mental exertion, visible in the veins popping out of his forehead.

Carmen still had a worried look on her face.

Majnun noticed a woman near a column admiring the Arabic inscriptions wearing a scarlet and yellow tunic, her face covered with a headscarf that allowed only her eyes to be seen. The woman possessed the modesty demanded by the Koran. But wasn't it immodest to wear that beautiful, expensive gold watch with precious stones on the wristband?

"She wants to take me to the secret chambers of the palace," he said.

"Who?" asked Carmen. "We're going this way. To the infirmary."

He recognized those eyes. The woman approaching him was Laila, released from her cat form. To find her, he had transported himself to a different time and come here. It would finally be possible to have her all to himself, and forever. He looked deep into her eyes. There was no doubt about it, they were impassioned eyes. He sensed that she was breathing heavily as she approached, with unhurried steps, bringing him tunic and turban. Suddenly, a doubt: might she be married, as she was when he knew her in that distant future? Should he take the initiative to kiss her? To embrace her?

"I think I've known you from long ago," he said carefully. "From a distant time in the future."

"Who are you talking to?" asked Carmen.

The woman smiled with her eyes alone, bashful. She muttered some mysterious sounds, which he understood with a profound, diffuse comprehension, impossible to express in words.

He closed his eyes, and the images of the woman continued to gnaw at his head, a soft gnawing, invisible, sensual particles, silent rhythms, images that lit up like a dim lantern, feeling their way through the darkness. He had chills, cold outside and hot inside, and then he trembled as if he were experiencing an earthquake. His entire life circulated through his veins. Words without thoughts provoked in him desire and misgiving, flowing like a river, one after another, in small waves, now kissing his forehead, now spitting in his face.

With his eyes still closed, he sat his backpack against the wall, took off his shirt, and put on the tunic and turban the woman had brought him. He felt dizzy again, he was going to fall, this time onto the hard ground.

Pablo and Carmen caught him.

"Where did Laila go?" he asked, opening his eyes to a brightness speckled with dark blotches.

"You're right, he's delirious," said Carmen in agreement with Pablo.

Another woman appeared, an older one. It was the Sultaness Aixa, Fátima, mother of Boabdil. A bitter woman, because her husband, Abul Hasan, had left her for Soraya. She stared at him with a severe look, as if asking for an explanation.

"My time has come," thought Majnun. He was in the middle of a crucial present where the future would be decided; faced with great events: the Byzantine Empire had already fallen into Muslim hands and America would be discovered in a few short years.

If Averroes had reintroduced Aristotle to Europe and thought up the double truth — the religiously revealed and the scientifically proven — he, Majnun, would be able, at the close of the fifteenth century, to do away with all religions, for if they weren't eliminated, they would bring about catastrophes in the following centuries. He couldn't remain indifferent. The desirable was possible. He would influence the destiny of the Iberian Peninsula and, therefore, of the world. Boabdil's cry hadn't existed yet and wouldn't have a reason to exist.

"I want to gather together my General Staff," he commanded, "to prevent the Catholic monarchs from defeating the sultan of Granada."

However, he had to be realistic: it wouldn't be possible to do away with all religions. He would have to invoke God. But what name would he give Him? Jehovah? Allah? One of the ninety and nine names of the God of the Koran? *Haqq*, which means truth or reality? Maybe the hundredth, the secret name only available to illuminated mystics?

There were many factors to consider. He mustn't take into account his own selfish interests, but rather what would be best for humanity. One thing was certain: he wasn't going to invoke Santiago, for there was no advantage to favoring the victory of the Catholic monarchs.

"Allahu Akbar," he said, adding: "Now that the general headquarters staff is assembled, we need to know exactly what year we are in. Could we still manage to keep Boabdil from becoming a prisoner and having to comply with the demands of Fernando and Isabel?"

"We're in 2011," clarified Carmen, trying to carve a path for their group amid a crowd of tourists.

"They're going to burn all the Arabic books in the Bib al-Rambla Plaza."

"They already burned them."

"They're going to forbid the Arabic language, customs, and religion. Muslims will be forced to become Moriscos, Mudejars, a domesticated, subjugated people."

"That already happened many centuries ago. And we're going to head back to the Albayzín soon, once you've been treated at the infirmary," said Carmen impatiently.

Majnun continued to talk, arousing the curiosity of passersby, a curiosity that was sharpened when they saw that he was wet, his face bloodied, his weight supported by two young women and a young man who were also completely soaked, Suzana's long white pants permitting a glimpse of her red panties, and Carmen's blouse, with no bra underneath, revealing her nipples.

"I've weighed all the consequences. Not even America will benefit from the victory of those monarchs. It isn't true that only the Catholic monarchs would send out the expedition of Christopher Columbus across the Mare Ignotum. He already tried to sell his plan to the Portuguese. He's been presenting his plan in vain to the Catholic monarchs since 1486. What year are we in, 1487? If it isn't accepted by the monarchs of Castile and Aragon, which can only happen if they win the war of Granada, he's ready to sell it to the French. And if the Catholic monarchs are defeated, he can very well undertake the expedition in the service of Granada."

In this case, the very name of "America" could be remedied, he thought. Indeed, because America got that name by mistake, as he'd read; because the cartographer Martin Waldseemüller, when he was designing his world map in 1507, a year after Columbus's death, believed that the new continent had been discovered by Amerigo Vespucci.

There was no doubt, the best option for the future of humanity was Islam, he continued to reflect. *Asslama, Sallama,* surrender yourself to God, obey His will, that there may be peace, *salam.* If Granada were the center of civilization today, the discovery of America would increase the progress of knowledge even more. For hadn't the Arabs fostered the study of pagan, Greek philosophy across the Peninsula, while the Christians refused to study anything that wasn't a religious text? Weren't they the ones who'd developed the discipline of medicine, while French doctors were trying to cure people on a basis of Christian superstitions?

"An intact Granada will shun decadence and allow the development of science," he said to the woman beside him, who appeared to be Carmen.

"He's gone crazy from one moment to the next," said Carmen quietly.

"Are you saying I've gone crazy just because I want to avoid this catastrophe? The Inquisition?" he protested. "Where's Boabdil?"

Carmen looked around them.

"We have to save Aarón," said Majnun, wiping off with his hand a trickle of blood that was running down his forehead. "If we do nothing, if we keep up this passivity, Granada is going to fall into the hands of the Catholic monarchs, and Aarón, like all the Jews, will be driven out. He'll have to leave his rosy house with balconies that look out onto a street in the Albayzín, with all of his family in tow, unless he converts or pretends to be a Christian. Either he'll be baptized or have to leave within four months, without the right to take any gold or silver with him. In his case, which I know well, this means an enormous loss."

"Aarón is a character in the novella he's writing," Carmen told Suzana.

"Where's Boabdil?" repeated Majnun. "Boabdil!" he shouted. "Aarón wants to go with you!"

Several French women turned around, curious, upon hearing the screams.

Boabdil was hiding or planning to escape, which he, Majnun, had to prevent at any cost. He would transform the destiny of Granada by informing Boabdil about what he had foreseen. Like Ibrahim, he could predict what was going to take place, but he didn't need a bronze ram or rooster. He'd google it, because fortunately his iPad was safe.

"Boabdil is a spirit that came down during the session we participated in at the Garden of Salvation," Carmen explained to Suzana as they went into the infirmary.

"Boabdil is here. Do you want to talk to me?" Majnun conjectured, looking at an approaching older man with a long beard like his and oddly disguised in a white robe, wearing neither his turban nor the rich red garments with black rosettes.

He looked closely into Boabdil's eyes and said:

"Remember that the world is in constant motion. As on a Ferris wheel, a person who is at the bottom one day can be on top the next; a person on top can be at the bottom the next day."

"*Hombre*, the wheel is very large; when the person at the bottom arrives at the top, he'll already be dead, *vale*?" said Pablo.

Suzana held back a laugh as Carmen elbowed her.

"Your spirit, if it is great, will survive. It will always be remembered. To live for the future, for the uncertain and the unknown; to communicate with the future through death . . . " said Majnun.

Then he pulled a card from his backpack and read:

"Titles and riches are not sufficient to honor a great man; nor punishment and degradation sufficient to dishonor him. He knows that between good and evil there is no absolute distinction. The man who possesses perfect virtue is not successful."

Exhausted, he sighed, tossed his backpack into a corner, and sat down on a chair. Then whispered:

"Not even heaven is perfect."

The man who thought he was Ibrahim

When Boabdil grabbed his wrist, Majnun asked:

"Didn't you dream about me, Sir?"

In the absence of a response, he asserted in a whisper:

"I am Ibrahim."

He took note of the sultan's apprehension and impatience. He didn't have a chessboard whose pieces moved all by themselves, but he could consult Google or download a film from YouTube on his iPad.

"I am Ibrahim, the oracle, who can foresee disasters and thus prevent them," he explained, raising his voice. "I am Ibrahim," he repeated. "Trust me. Eliminate all useless anguish and dreamy hope."

He pointed the iPad in another direction to get better reception.

"How about your iPad? Is it also from the Middle Ages?" asked Pablo, walking over to him.

"This is no time for jokes," objected Carmen.

"If we're in the year 888 of the Hijra or 1483 of the Gregorian calendar, you can't trust in the ability of Aliatar to defend you," said Majnun to Boabdil, referring to the sultan's father-in-law, Moraima's father, governor of Loja. "Above all else, do not recruit troops from Loja. You, Sir, will be defeated and imprisoned in Loja, and your father-in-law will be killed."

"Boabdil can't have much experience as a sultan, since he's only been sultan for a short while," thought Majnun, who believed himself to be Ibrahim.

"He's very sensitive. Believe what I said: he could be seeing spirits that we can't see," insisted Carmen, whispering in Suzana's ear.

"We can control the situation from the observatory in the Hall of Ambassadors, over on the other side of the pool," asserted Majnun.

"Hand me my saddlebag," he ordered Carmen, referring to his backpack.

He pulled out another card:

"Carry out that which you are brought to carry out, without concern for what will happen; for he who fulfills his obligation without worrying about the result will achieve supreme good."

Boabdil took his pulse and put a stethoscope to his chest. Finally, with the help of a medic, he dressed the wound on his forehead.

Without taking his eyes off him, Majnun continued. He was now speaking in a measured tone and demonstrated knowledge and a capacity for reason, only faltering in rational argumentation because he got the century mixed up:

"You, Sir, should fight without hope, without selfishness, and free of all anguish. Do not trust Queen Isabel and King Fernando. They won't fulfill their promise to respect the customs of the vanquished. If you surrender in 1492 and receive a guarantee that, according to the terms of agreement, Muslims who wish to stay in Granada will be able to continue practicing their religion, don't believe it. It's a pure lie. Intolerance will grow starting in 1499, mainly because of the Franciscan fanatic, the queen's confessor and future Inquisitor-General of Castile, Friar Francisco Jiménez de Cisneros. Under his influence, they'll initiate the forced conversion of four thousand Muslims in Granada. They'll banish the Sephardic Jews and the Moriscos, and persecute the gypsies. All of this to say that you, Sir, can't put off the implementation of your war plans until the last minute. Everything has to be done well in advance. This is the strategy. Act now in anticipation of what is predicted to happen in 1492: provoke an uprising from here to the sea and seek reinforcements from the Muslim princes of North Africa."

"The problem is that these reinforcements will never arrive. It was only a rumor that the Mameluk sultan of Egypt threatened King Fernando if he ever invaded Granada and that the Turks and the Maghrebis were going to join forces with the Egyptians. Boabdil will have to surrender," replied Pablo, as if he seriously wanted to debate with a crazy person. Then, turning to Suzana, he explained: "Actually, his surrender saved Granada and the Alhambra, which the Catholic monarchs would have destroyed, as they did with Málaga in 1487."

Majnun reflected on what he'd heard and then said, very softly:

"It was in the spring of 1487 that those Catholic monarchs began the conquest of Málaga."

He had to acknowledge the impossible. "Knowing what we can do nothing to stop and accepting this impossibility as our destiny, this is the supreme virtue. " He read this line from one of the cards in his backpack. Maybe by now the Muslim sovereigns of Fez and Tlemcen had already sent their messages, accompanied with presents, to King Fernando, promising never to take up arms against him. Had he, Majnun, arrived in Granada too late? Were they already in the final day of the month of Safar in 897 of the Hijra, the beginning of the Christian year 1492? Perhaps King Fernando had already ordered taking hostage of five hundred representatives of the most important families of Granada until his troops peacefully occupied the city. Majnun felt profound anguish, frowned, and hunched over. Then his eyes filled with tears.

"They never should have started buying peace with the Christians through taxes," he said, sobbing.

Boabdil and the entire court around him were now laughing.

Majnun recognized Suzana, who was squeezing his arm now and then. She was one of his wives. He didn't love her, but here marriage wasn't done out of love. Polygamy was normal, and three wives were enough for him: in addition to Suzana, Carmen and Laila, who had brought him a shawl. They fulfilled three of his necessities. Carmen was affectionate and took care of him. He was in love with Laila. And he could repudiate Suzana when the lust wore off and trade her in for someone else.

Yet he had a vague recollection of Suzana cheating on him. Of course, with Pablo, the Spaniard, now he remembered it clearly. She should be stoned to death.

"Where is Pablo? I need to challenge him to a duel."

"Why?" asked Carmen, relieved to see that he was starting to recognize his friends.

"It's a matter of honor. Because one of my wives spent the night with him. The two of them must die. Honor must be honored."

"No. You're delirious," said Carmen, trying again to bring him back to reality.

Majnun heard noises, whispers, voices muttering incomprehensible phrases . . . Where were they going? They walked down a main road, he and his friends, as well as Boabdil, who wanted to accompany them so he could show them something extraordinary. They walked through a gate, which everyone stopped to admire.

"The key and the hand that I sculpted myself," said Majnun, pointing to the top of the gate, which they would soon pass through again, he with saddlebag on his shoulders and wineskin on his hip.

Boabdil was walking beside him. Laila was walking up front, Majnun recognized her now. Atop a white horse, she was dressed as a gothic princess, covered in jewels and with a silver lyre pendant hanging from her neck which shone in the sun and blinded his eyes. The Gate of Justice did exist, it was there. Majnun noticed that Boabdil, as Aben Habuz had done centuries earlier, looked towards the towers and gardens of the Alhambra without being able to see them.

"You, Sir, will only be able to see the palace and its gardens after you pass through the enchanted gate," Majnun proclaimed.

He pointed at the hand and the key once more.

"Those are the talismans that guard the entrance to this paradise. As long as the hand doesn't fall down onto the key, no power will prevail over you, Sir, or the Alhambra. Trust in me, I am Ibrahim."

"He's getting better. He's reasoning now," Carmen whispered to Suzana.

Majnun — that is, Ibrahim — now saw Princess Laila in the gateway, in the exact center of the barbican.

"Stop," he said, when Laila began to pass through the Gate of Justice. "I now have a right to my reward. You, Sir, promised me, in exchange for the protection of Granada, the load carried by the first animal to enter through this magical gate. The princess is mine. That is all I want in exchange for what I've given you. Nothing more. Reign in your kingdom. I am going with Laila to my philosophical retreat."

He then ran towards Laila, who perhaps had some mascara on, for she looked different. She was wearing a short white dress, instead of her medieval garb, but her green eyes were the same as the cat's, the same as the Laila who had brought him the tunic. His payment for being the new Ibrahim and preventing the destruction of Granada had finally arrived. He couldn't resist: he squeezed both of Laila's breasts with zeal and, as he went to kiss her, was violently restrained by Boabdil. Was Boabdil in love with Laila, as when Sultan Aben Habuz had been in love with the beautiful Christian prisoner, daughter of Gothic princes?

He realized his mistake too late: he would sit in judgment, for the woman he thought was Laila was actually Sultaness Moraima, Boabdil's wife. How hadn't he noticed that that long, black hair couldn't be Laila's? He would be sentenced to death by the tribunal gathered near the Gate of Justice, where many people were congregated, some of them eating ice cream, others with glasses of wine in their hands, people from the future, typical twenty-first-century tourists, who laughed at him, noisy people who lacked the respectability of the Moorish period and were dressed in inappropriate attire. In the shop nearby, there were sacrilegious figures for sale, which represented human and animal forms. The slackening of Islamic morals was corrupting Granada. The hatred towards women who didn't sufficiently cover themselves would grow; as would the hatred towards men who drank the wine imported from Málaga and other forbidden drinks.

Boabdil was wholly reasonable in wanting to defend his honor. And what about him, Majnun? Didn't he have honor to defend? He became filled with hatred.

"I don't deserve death, I'm not worthy of it yet," he announced, irate. "Death demands of me a grandiose act. I need to challenge the Spaniard to a duel. Where's Pablo?" he asked again.

"*Hombre*, I'm right here," replied Pablo.

Majnun tried to take the Swiss Army knife out of his backpack, but a uniformed man brusquely prevented him.

"Before you execute me, allow me to give you all some counsel: your only salvation is in accompanying Boabdil to Fez," he said, looking at his three travel companions, as well as Aarón, Boabdil's

Jewish interpreter, whom he could now make out in the middle of the crowd.

"What do you mean? Didn't you save Granada?" asked Pablo with a smile.

"You really do deserve to be executed," said Suzana with finality.

"Fleeing to Fez isn't going to work out," continued Pablo. "We are all under suspicion. We stand in solidarity with you," he said, addressing Majnun.

"Don't do that," said Carmen, reprimanding the others.

"Look here, Majnun, I can make predictions too: first, Boabdil, still regarded as a prince, just not a prince of Granada, will take possession of a fiefdom in the Alpujarras, but, soon after the death of Moraima, he is going to depart from the port of Adra in October of 1493, along with his mother Aixa and an enormous retinue, for Fez. His sister will stay behind in Spain and have a son with King Fernando, the Catholic."

At the moment when Majnun thought that a sword was going to slice through his neck, two policemen detained him. He had time to grab his iPad, where he saw new emails, one from Laila with the subject line "good news" and another from his grandma Elvira about his grandpa. He had enough time to read the subject lines, but not to read the emails themselves, for the policemen quickly confiscated his iPad.

His friends objected. He was being arrested for public disturbance and brandishing a knife, explained the policemen, who then asked to see everyone's identification. Following a brief dispute, the three Brazilians were taken to an immigration detention center. Pablo went with them, out of solidarity, still objecting in vain against the arbitrariness of their detention.

Carmen and Suzana presented their documents and were free to go.

"I had my documents," explained Majnun, "but I left them in the Middle Ages."

He had a dim recollection of that distant past, which in some way defined and influenced his emotions.

"You're not going to be able to return to the past, but take a look at your future: you can be confined to this place for the next eighteen months, even with no sentence," said the policeman, irritated at what seemed like a joke to him. Later, as if out of regret for what he'd said, he added: "The most likely thing is that you'll be deported soon. That's the best thing for you."

"Don't you worry, my friend," said Carmen. "We'll find a lawyer. You'll be out of here very soon and you can stay with me in Madrid."

"Take the wallet that's in my backpack. There's money in there," Majnun told her.

What's the use of living

A month and a half later, in Madrid, Carmen invited Suzana to a sherry bar called La Venencia on Calle de Echegaray, near the Plaza de Santa Ana. She wanted to clear up a misunderstanding. Suzana had broken up with Pablo, supposedly because of her, and had stopped speaking to her.

Ancient posters adorned the walls of the darkened bar. On the other side of the counter, standing in front of a number of casks of sherry, the bartender explained the differences between several varieties: *fino, manzanilla, oloroso, palo cortado*, and *amontillado*. Carmen sampled an *oloroso* and finally settled on the *palo cortado*. Suzana opted for a *fino*.

They sat down at a table in the back with their glasses of sherry and a saucer of green olives. No sooner had they finished their sherries, than Carmen began to cry. She confessed to Suzana that she was pregnant.

"You can tell me. I already know. It's Pablo's kid, isn't it?"

Before the trip to Granada, Suzana had noticed Carmen sneaking off, disappearing for hours at a time without saying where she was going. Carmen had known Pablo in Brasilia, demonstrated knowledge of details about his family, and had stayed at his father's apartment.

"Tell me the truth. I need to know. It's Pablo's kid, isn't it?" she repeated.

"It's his father's, Rodrigo's."

"His father's? Have you gone crazy?"

"It went down that very first night."

"But do you like him?"

"It's complicated. I'm starting to realize that I think of him as my grandfather."

"Your grandfather?"

Carmen looked up at the top of the wall, then towards the door. She wrinkled up her brow between eyes brimming with tears.

"My grandfather abused me when I was a child," she said, now sobbing. She took a handkerchief out of her purse to dry her eyes.

"And you never reported him?" said Suzana, taking hold of Carmen's hands.

"He was the only one who treated me kindly."

"Are you going to have the baby?"

"I don't know."

"Are you going to stay in that crazy relationship?"

"I don't know about that either. Oh, my friend, my life is super fucked up."

"Pablo is going to Brazil," said Suzana.

"Are you two going together?"

"We're taking a break. He says he's going to look for work, maybe in São Paulo. But he isn't going to apply for a visa, which I think is risky. He's entering through Fortaleza as a tourist, on a flight from Lisbon on TAP Airlines. As for me, I'm going back to Brasilia. I shouldn't have even stayed here this long. We'll see what ends up happening. It was going well at first . . . I'm Catholic, he isn't, but the problem was that, deep down, he's more Catholic than I am. It's such a Catholic thing when certain men can no longer have fun with their girlfriends once the relationship gets serious and they start to see them as their future wives. They only know how to have fun with lovers. Although who knows, maybe I was unfair with him. I suspected that Pablo might have a lover on the side. And, I'm sorry to say, I could've sworn it was you."

"Majnun has been released. He's coming to Madrid and is going to stay with me," Carmen informed her. "Rodrigo kicked me out of the apartment when I suggested that Majnun could share a room with me. 'It's either him or me,' he told me. 'Why are you so jealous?' I asked him. 'You said yourself that he's the only man you're interested in,' he replied. 'Yes,' I explained to him, 'but I also said that he's not interested in me and that nothing is going to happen between us.' 'Me or him,' he kept repeating. There was no way around it, and I lost my patience. I ended up telling him that I preferred Majnun. 'Do I mean nothing to you?' he asked me. At which point I opened up to him and confessed what I just told you, that I see him as my grandfather. Then things got bad fast. It got so damn ugly. Now I'm renting a room here in Lavapiés."

"I found out a little something about this whole story with Majnun through a phone call from my dad. He and Majnun's grandpa, Dario, met each other the time that Majnun disappeared here in Madrid. Now they've stayed in contact. Majnun's finally going back to Brasilia, isn't he?"

"Yep. His situation might have been all cleared up. The police have another suspect in the murder of Laila's husband. A car thief who had stolen some cars in the area. The suspect denies it, though, and didn't even steal Laila's husband's car. But all the evidence points to him, there were fingerprints, the type of bullet matches his revolver . . . Who knows? My theory is that when he encountered resistance, he fired at him, but then had to run off quickly for some reason. And Majnun is back in contact with Laila. This is still the main problem: he can't stop thinking about her. Another complication is that he isn't convinced by the police investigation. He thinks he's guilty. He says he's not going to let an innocent man go to jail in his place. He wants to turn himself in when he gets to Brazil. Oh, I wanted to ask you something: can you accompany Majnun on the trip back to Brasilia?"

"He treated me very badly," said Suzana, without going into detail.

"It's because he was sick. But I'm certain he's better now. I even think he's completely recovered. It was just an episode. He won't cause you any problems."

"I don't know."

"What's the use of living, if you aren't willing to die for something? What's the point of a life without heroism, without sacrifice, a life that's content with comfort and consumption, with the prolonging of life itself? Think about it: What cause would you die for right now? For country? For religion? For an ideology?" Majnun asked Carmen as she was taking him to the Consulate General of Brazil, on Calle Zurbano, to try to get a travel document that would allow him to return to Brazil.

"I'd die for my child, if it required my life in order to survive," replied Carmen. "I found out I'm pregnant."

"But that's not even necessary, you don't have to risk your life for your child," he said, not seeming surprised at the news.

"If it was necessary . . ."

"But it isn't."

"Rodrigo's the father. I'm going to have it here and I intend to stay in Madrid. It won't be the first time I've had to make it on my own somewhere. Despite the fight we had, Rodrigo says that he'll recognize the child as his, register it as our child."

"Are you going to marry that guy?"

"We already broke up."

"And did you want a kid?"

"What matters is that I want it now and it's what I want most in this world. There's one thing: I used a little of your money, but don't worry, I'll pay you back."

"Don't worry about it."

At the Consulate, an employee explained that it wouldn't be possible to process the passport unless Majnun had his original birth certificate or a Brazilian national ID card.

"Listen here, you don't understand. They're trying to kill me, I'm being followed," he said, raising his voice.

"Calm down, calm down. We're going to help you," said the young woman at the counter.

"I lost my documents, but they exist, and you all should be able to track down a copy. They want to execute me because I mistook Moraima for Laila. They're still after me, trying to kill me. If I die, it's your fault."

The employee explained that she could issue an Authorization of Return to Brazil. While she prepared the document, she directed them to the Consular Assistance Division. In a small room, a vice-consul, after hearing Majnun's stories about Laila, Moraima, Boabdil, and the persecution he was suffering, suggested contacting a psychiatric hospital, where Majnun could stay until he left for Brazil.

"No, that's not necessary," said Carmen, thanking her. "He's going to stay with me and will travel to Brazil in the company of a friend."

And truly, Carmen still held out hope of convincing Suzana to travel with Majnun.

It was already autumn. Majnun left Madrid on a TAP flight at eight-thirty at night on a Saturday and, because of the difference in time zones, arrived in Lisbon at about the same time. After a three-hour layover in Portela de Sacavém airport, he boarded a direct flight to Brasilia.

At seven-thirty in the morning on Sunday, when the plane landed in Brasilia, he awoke from a dream: he was lying with Suzana on a pile of cushions in the corner of a room of the Alhambra, and Laila was watching over them with a sparkling stare from a church pulpit, which was oddly out of place in the Alhambra.

Majnun trembled from a mix of pleasure and fear when he spotted the city's skyline from the plane window. There were no clouds in the sky, and the brightness hurt his eyes.

He hadn't written a single line of his novella in some time. He pulled a bunch of crumpled papers out of his backpack. He wrote down whatever came to mind, and what came to mind was Laila and a passion that had weathered the storms and could now grow in the subsequent calm. He tried to recall his medieval Spanish past, but only a shadow of it remained. He composed the end of his novella, writing of a love that withstands absence, misunderstandings, and even the loved one's rejection. He kept writing until the flight attendant broke his concentration:

"Aren't you getting off?"

Nothing is perfect, everything is possible

There were a lot of cars in front of his grandparents' house, the doors of which were open and full of people.

When he entered, backpack on his shoulders, the housemaid, a Pernambucan woman with a gaunt face and curly blond hair, gave him a hug, a rosary between her fingers:

"We've been waiting for you, my son. Thank goodness you arrived in time."

His grandma Elvira broke out into tears when she saw him. She embraced him. And then Majnun began to cry profusely. Down his face ran tears of sorrow, not only for having lost the most precious thing he had, his grandpa Dario, the grandpa he'd abandoned and disobeyed, but also tears of hopelessness for being nothing, desiring nothing, not knowing who he was or who he could be. His grandma Mona, also present, came over to hug him.

"Sérgio couldn't make it," she said.

The body of his grandpa Dario was laid out in the coffin, surrounded by friends. Spirits really exist, thought Majnun, and his grandfather's spirit existed too. It was all that was left of him, the collection of memories he left behind, all of this would remain forever as he reached his final destination. There were people who, even after they were dead, continued to connect one person to the next, uniting humanity in a common purpose. Grandpa Dario would be one of them. Majnun observed the body of the deceased, wrapped in a black shroud, the solemn coffin surrounded by four candelabras, the flowers from which emanated a scent of death and sadness. The state of celestial peace in which his grandfather lay wasn't any sort of peace at all. It only brought uneasiness.

He wanted to escape those cruel, unacceptable surroundings. He looked into the casket once more. A bee flitted around the flowers. If it stung his grandpa's hands or lips, that inert body would feel no pain. No, his grandpa wasn't that lifeless body, that pale flesh that would decompose, start to stink, of which only the bones would remain, though, with the passage of time, perhaps even they would disappear. His grandma Elvira was sobbing now, sobs that were perhaps brought on by Majnun's expression as he stood in front of the casket, but he, Majnun, couldn't summon tears from that mixture of anger and guilt. He shooed the bee away with his hand.

Suzana arrived with her parents. They hugged Dona Elvira, who led them over to the small circle of people around the deceased who were praying the rosary. When she saw Majnun, Suzana took pity on him. He seemed so different than the crude guy who had nearly raped her. She noticed the visible fragility in his eyes and even felt a tenderness towards him.

While they were preparing to leave for the cemetery, Majnun turned to his grandma Mona:

"I still don't know what to do."

"About what?"

"I don't know if I want to convert. I'm not fully convinced . . ."

"Look, in Islam there's this concept called *ijtihad*, which means personal diligence, independent reasoning, or the effort of pondering on your own. Trust, therefore, in your own reason. And the Koran says to be firm in the observance of justice, acting as a witness of God out of love, even if you are witnessing despite yourself, your parents, or your relatives. That's is the most important thing."

His most recent readings for the essay on tolerance he was going to include in his novella had left him confused. He had analyzed the position of the Koran in relation to Judaism and Christianity. Some verses accepted the Jews; in others, the language about Jews was hostile and considered them to have distorted the words of Scripture, forgotten a large part of what had been revealed to them, and didn't deem them true believers, only a very few among them. One verse said to pardon them and forgive their errors, for God esteems the well-doer. Majnun had understood, from reading other verses, that there was a clear preference for Christians, since they were closer in affection to the believers and were never prideful about anything. Tears had even flowed from their eyes when they heard what had been revealed to the Messenger. But, according to another passage, neither Christians nor Jews should be taken as trusted friends.

Should he ask his grandma Mona to clarify these issues or was he no longer interested in knowing about any of that?

"I wanted to believe, but . . ." he muttered.

"It is written in the Book, let there be no compulsion in religion; so whoever wills, let him believe, and whoever wills, let him disbelieve; and had Allah willed, He would have made you one nation."

"So is there tolerance towards atheists?" he asked, since, despite all his interest in Islam, he still saw himself as the spiritual heir of his grandpa Dario, an atheist.

"Judge for yourself from those verses, as well as what another one says: 'And had your Lord willed, those on earth would have believed, all of them entirely. Then, O Mohammed, would you compel the people in order that they become believers?'"

Mona waited for Majnun's reaction. But he remained pensive, silent, little convinced by what she'd said.

"What I can tell you with complete certainty," she continued, "is that Islam has respect for the people of the Book, all of them monotheists. It is written that they shouldn't argue with followers of the Book, except in the best manner possible, because Muslims also believe in what was revealed to the prophets before Mohammed. And there is but one God, and we all submit to Him. It's true that one verse says that whoever desires to impose a religion that isn't Islam will be among the losers. Many exegetes claim that this verse abrogates another: the one that dictates that Christians, Jews — anyone who believes in God and practices righteous good deeds — will have nothing to fear and will receive their divine reward. But others claim that both verses are valid. Compare all that with the Catholics! They had to wait until the Second Vatican Council to abandon the principle that there is no salvation outside the Catholic Church. Even in the Middle Ages, in Al-Andalus, when it was governed by Muslim law, priests and rabbis, as well as their churches and synagogues, were protected, and the ecclesiastical and rabbinical tribunals were authorized to apply their own laws. We're all a part of the same

Islamo-Judeo-Christian ethical and metaphysical universe."

And what if they weren't people of the Book, Majnun wanted to know. His grandma then cited the example of Akbar, the third Mughal emperor of India, a Muslim who reigned from 1556 to 1605 and started a movement of rapprochement with Hinduism, even marrying a Hindu woman.

At the cemetery, Majnun moved away from the group, his grandma, and Suzana and walked among the trees. He left the cemetery, walked passed the gardens of the houses along the W3, and went down towards the "super square" apartment complexes. On the horizon, which he could see above the scissor-shaped on-ramps to the Eixão highway, the difference between sky and earth, between hill and cloud was dissolving, as in a painting by Guignard. He imagined robbing a bank, getting drunk on every imaginable kind of booze, getting high on the best drugs, breaking down the door to Laila's house in the middle of the night, abducting her like guys used to do in the old days, taking her to live with him, swimming with her under a waterfall, both of them naked, getting lost on the highways with her, challenging any man who got close to her to a duel, he would kill him, he, the hero of himself, the hero of that relationship of love, no, not of love, of passion, a perennial passion. Why had she once again stopped replying to his emails and messages on Facebook?

He walked through the "super square" complexes at random. He felt weak, as if his legs could no longer support him, his arms carry no more weight, nor his tongue pronounce a single word. He walked without rhythm, as if the ground couldn't hold onto him and he were just a shadow trying to mimic his own gestures.

Someone waved at him and laughed, but it didn't seem like a real person. Maybe it was an animal of some unknown species. It wasn't talking to him, but to some ghost, someone from a different time, a different century. He picked up his pace, not wanting to talk to anyone.

He smelled the scent of the city in the air. It was space, more than time, that had the power to transport him to another world, far from his immediate concerns. The power to free him, to reunite him with a primitive purity. Instead of escaping to somewhere else, he should take a highway with no fixed route.

The "super square" complex remained in the same spot, with its church in front of the "interblock," where the shops were located. He had to return to a time in which things happened all by themselves, opening up onto an infinite world where everything was possible.

Humans die equals

To remember, to remember—*recordar*, to pass once more through the heart. What he could perceive from his state of madness was something like a memory of his lucidity. Yes, it was better to return to his own life. To Laila. Laila, who was truth, reality.

He thought about abandoning his novella and what he'd written of the essay. Why try to resuscitate stories of intolerant people persecuted by even more intolerant people? He didn't have the head for anything anymore, except for Laila. He had never stopped loving her during those months and he would love her forever. He loved her with a desire and hatred that were equally intense. He had a passion for her that was unscrupulous, like all passions, a font of inexhaustible unease.

He sent her a message:

"I'm back in Brasilia."

This time she replied: "Welcome home."

A good sign. He urgently needed to see her. Nothing like physical presence to test one's love. In her presence, his heart pounded endlessly. In her absence, a piece of him died. Laila was a widow now; she had no reason to reject him.

He now dared to tell her what he hadn't had the courage to say up to this point. He would know how to seduce her, kiss her, hold her in his arms, even though his arms had lost all strength. He would forgive her for the sorrow she had caused him. And if she rejected him? All or nothing. He would kill Laila and commit suicide. He thought about going back to the place where he'd buried the revolver beneath the cashew tree. No, there was no time for that. He would strangle Laila with his bare hands, which mortal hatred would make strong.

He walked over to the bus station and from there took a bus to the Lago Norte neighborhood. It was hot out, and he was sweating. He wiped sweat from his forehead several times. Through the window, the vegetation was as dry as his soul. People were talking to each other beside him, others were talking on their cell phones, voices intermingled with the sounds of the bus.

He recognized the stop where he needed to get off, the deserted streets, and, finally, the house that backed up against the lakefront. Did Laila still live there? Would she be glad to see him? The lake trembled with fear.

He rang the doorbell. No one answered. He thought about walking around the house to see if there was an open window or door, or one he could force open. He decided against it. Dejection fell over him. He sat down on the doorstep. He was about to head back to the highway when a maid opened the door, and back behind her he saw Laila in a red robe. The closer she came to him, the older she looked. Her smile revealed wrinkles all around her mouth. A natural Laila, without makeup, her hair uncombed, beauty in its natural state.

She didn't resist his embrace.

"I've come to stay with you forever," he said.

She invited him in. They went into the living room. He sat down near the window, which let in that same bright light he'd seen from the airplane which had hurt his eyes.

"Something to drink?" she asked.

"Water."

After handing him a glass of water, she sat down beside him:

"I need to tell you that I'm in love. I have a boyfriend."

She spoke with tenderness in her voice and a quiver in her lips. She also spoke like the much older woman she was, and as if she were addressing the adolescent that he was.

Those words, and principally the manner in which they were spoken, were like a sharpened, cold dagger thrust into Majnun's heart. He constrained himself, but his facial expression changed. The silence was easy to read. It said more than a chaotic accumulation of words.

No, it wasn't possible that Laila preferred someone else, just like that. Was he going to lose her because he didn't know how to win when challenged by another person? He thought about what he'd determined to do: strangle her and then commit suicide. Instead of this, he pulled from his pocket some crumpled papers, on which he had written a glorious ending to his novella as the plane was landing in Brasilia.

"Read them," he said. "They're for you."

She read silently and unhurriedly, while he examined her facial expressions, trying to obtain from them some sign of hope.

"Very beautiful. You've got real talent," she said, like an insensitive teacher.

She handed the papers back to him with a polite smile.

"You're young and have your whole future in front of you. I'm not the right person for you," she said, running her hand through his hair.

Majnun pushed her hand away. He stood up and, without another word to her, ran towards the door. Disoriented, he started walking down the street. The mistake had been for her to get close to him out of passion, he thought, a woman fifteen years older than him. A huge mistake, for nothing can endure if it rests upon something volatile, something that evaporates, carried off by fire and wind and, just as suddenly as it arrives, it soon disappears.

A mistake? What bullshit! The illusionist that resided within him and manipulated his thoughts soon found a way to negate the idea that such a passion would have to end, for if that were the case, how could one explain why his passion for Laila didn't evaporate, why, instead of being carried off by fire and wind, it was an unending fire, stoked by the wind?

He came across a family—a woman, a man, two adolescent daughters, and a boy who was, at most, eight years old—who kept him company on the deserted street. The sultry air provoked sorrow in his soul. There was also sorrow in that family. It was visible and, more than just visible, it was almost possible to touch it. The man looked at him with an interested expression, which made Majnun feel both odd and attracted. One of the adolescent girls exchanged a glance with him. She had rouge on her black cheeks and was wearing a skirt printed with small blue flowers. On her shoulders, the straps of a black bra. The other one, wearing very worn out pants, looked serious as she walked, perhaps bored. Majnun matched his pace to the man's and asked him:

"Are you all from here?"

"We're from Goiás."

"Do you know where the police station is?"

"No, I don't."

"I need to go to the police station."

"Were you assaulted?"

"No, it's just that I need to turn myself in."

"You seem like a good person. You don't have the face of someone who needs to turn himself in to the police," said the man.

"I think I killed a guy."

"You think you did?"

"Yeah. An innocent man might have been sent to prison in my place."

The man, woman, the two adolescents, and the boy all started moving away from him, avoiding the company of that possible criminal or perhaps just needing to head in a different direction.

Majnun walked under the hot sun, alone. While the world was disappearing, he was disappearing . . . Every once in a while he remembered: he was going to turn himself in to the police. Now he was certain: an innocent man had gone to jail in his place, and he could not allow that. Never! An enormous sense of guilt came over him. Guilt at having allowed an innocent man to pay for the crime in his stead. Guilt that gnawed at him from the inside. He was the worst of all men. He deserved to go to prison, deserved much more than prison. Guilt, too, about feeling guilty. And what if he spent years in prison? He needed that, to pay for his guilt, for a lot of guilt; to remain locked away in prison, separated from the rest of the world. He consulted Google on his iPhone, which continued to function because the account had never stopped being paid by automatic withdrawal. The Ninth Precinct Police Station was only two kilometers away, at most.

The sun was burning his face, and he was sweating so much that his shirt was drenched. He took off his shirt and stuck it in his waistband and kept going, naked from the waist up. He saw himself in a Holy Week procession, performing penance, whipping himself, blood dripping down his back, atoning for that guilt that had invaded his entire being. His blood pressure fell, and he felt like he was going to faint. With much effort and after a long walk, he arrived at the police station.

"I'm here because I committed a murder," he said, sincere and breathless, seeing blotches in his field of vision as he propped his arms on the counter.

The policeman didn't look surprised.

"Do you have ID?"

"I did. A document that the Consulate gave me. But I handed it over at the airport."

"Fill out this form."

While Majnun examined the form, the policeman, sitting down in front of the computer, asked him:

"What are you confessing to?"

"I killed my girlfriend's husband and hid the revolver at the place where I was working."

"What's the address?"

"Parkway Region, Block 50, Complex 1. The revolver is beneath a cashew tree."

The policeman listened dispassionately to Majnun as he explained that, after sleepwalking out of his house at night and dreaming that he'd killed Laila's husband, he had found a revolver under his pillow, and that, in Madrid, he had also seen a bloody knife under his pillow, though it later disappeared, perhaps Carmen or Suzana, with whom he was sharing a room, had hidden it.

"What's your address?"

Majnun gave him his address in the Dom Bosco Mansions neighborhood.

"Phone number?"

He gave him his cell phone number.

The policeman jotted it all down.

"Sign here," he said.

"Aren't you going to arrest me?"

"We have your contact information. If necessary, we'll be in touch."

On the form, the policeman added that Majnun looked crazy or drugged-out.

Walking along the edge of the Parque Peninsula North Highway, sun on his face, Majnun jumped from one thought to the next, one misgiving to the next. His turbulent life was in constant motion. Every time he tried to detain it, to comprehend it, life escaped him again. Nothing was stable in this life; people were always just passing through. They didn't stick around to tell their stories. Not even Laila.

In that desert, which could take him in a variety of directions, he didn't feel free, but abandoned. In the middle of the vortex of ideas swirling inside his head, one got caught in a corner of his brain: he was going to die. Death appeared to him in various forms. First, it came to asphyxiate him, and the air that was lacking was love. This was how he would die: from a lack of love. Not only because Laila didn't love him, but also because he himself would never be able to love anyone else.

Then, cold and distant, death merely watched as he committed suicide. He was going to kill himself because he was no longer able to imagine or write a single line of his novella, whose ending had made no impression on Laila. And if he didn't kill himself, death—that impartial tyrant, cold and disrespectful, who didn't discriminate and suddenly barged into a life like a virus—would come anyway, decapitating him with its scythe in some accident. He was always thinking about tragic accidents.

He finally understood why Laila had sent him that postcard with a reproduction of *La belle Rosine* on it. Majnun looked into his own eyes in the reflection on the screen of his iPhone. He was Rosine. The same skeleton in the mirror. Laila's premonition.

It wasn't true that all men were born equal, he thought. What was certain was that they died equal, they turned to dust, dust that was the same for both rich and poor. "Time transforms all of humanity into dust," he said aloud. "That is what I am: potential dust, nothing more." He should face death with honor. Perfection existed; it existed in death, the perfect conclusion. The hour had come. He was crawling around in the mud like a humiliated animal. In truth, he already felt dead. He wasn't resting in peace, but in agony.

A car braked beside him, its tires squealing on the asphalt. Two guys got out of it.

"I recognize this asshole," said one of them. "You're the son of a bitch who gave us that dead dog as a present."

"Wake up, dude, this is a kidnapping," said the other.

"Again?" replied Majnun.

The two men immobilized him and laid him down in the backseat of the car. One of the criminals held a gun to his ear, while the other was putting a blindfold on him.

"Hand over your wallet, we're going to the bank to withdraw cash."

"I don't have any money. Or a credit card."

"Call your dad."

"He's dead."

"Then call your mom, you dumbass."

"She's institutionalized. She can't answer the phone."

"Stop playing around, you son of a bitch. You trying to get yourself killed?"

"Yes, I am. It's all I think about."

"Oh yeah? Let's take this asshole to that place."

Heading towards Lago Norte, they took a side road. At an isolated locale, they walked Majnun down into the trees and tied him to a tree trunk.

"We're gonna take some target practice until you decide to cooperate," said one of the criminals.

Majnun was startled by a shot that went between his legs, very nearly hitting him. He felt the wind of another bullet in his hair, this one lodging in the tree above his head. Other shots followed.

All of a sudden, he heard the sound of the criminals running towards their car and taking off in a rush. Then the sound of approaching footsteps.

"Lucky guy," a policeman told him as he removed his blindfold.

Majnun looked at him with shock, full of that interest in life that proximity to death instills in the living. He discovered that he had an objective that was much more ambitious than dying: never dying, to fake out death, to be eternal. And further: to live forever at the age of twenty. As someone once said, pessimism of the intellect is the optimism of will.

Only by being eternal, knowing the totality of things, would it be possible to think with a lucidity that was more than fleeting, conditioned by the time period and worried about the future. Live eternally in order to do everything, correct what needed to be corrected, complete what needed to be completed. Which is to say, in order to be perfect. Perfect? Perfection was just a distant beacon. "Reason can go to hell. Reason is controlling, bossy. No, I don't want to be perfect, I prefer to be alive."

The policemen took him back to the Ninth Precinct Station. The policeman who had questioned him earlier was no longer there. Another one took his statement about what had happened, writing down in detail the description he gave of his kidnappers.

He regretted not having a friend to tell about what he'd been through in the last few hours. His virtual friends were bubbles, like the ones in the stock market, which burst and disappeared, leaving behind only debts, crises, and solitude. With his grandpa Dario dead, he was a solitary planet, floating freely, without a star to orbit. He had Carmen, his one romantic hope. But Carmen was far away.

Suzana had given him her phone number. Might she pick up?

"I've been worried about you. How are you feeling?"

"Doing well, very well. Want to go out some day?" he asked abruptly.

"Yes, let's go out, some day."

"What about today?"

"Why don't you come by the house?"

He got off the bus at ERW South Road and went on foot to Suzana's apartment. The blue sky was still overhead, dotted here and there with sparse clouds, which calmly glided above the buildings. The whiteness of the city contrasted with those green walls, rows of trees in front of the windows of the buildings. In the distance—perhaps in the central square of one of the "super square" complexes—he could hear a concert, though he couldn't pick out any instruments other than electric guitars.

Majnun took the elevator to Suzana's floor together with a group of adolescents, two girls and a boy, who talked incessantly until they got off at their floor, the fourth floor. He went up to the sixth, where Suzana lived with her parents.

He greeted Suzana with a propriety and discretion that were new to him, almost as if they were unknown. Only after she offered her cheek to him did he greet her with a kiss, though he didn't touch his lips to hers.

She was wearing a blue blouse with vertical pleats and a brown skirt with pockets on the backside. She had put her long blond hair up into a ponytail and she gave off a scent of perfume that he recognized. She crossed the living room with an elegant lightness that was unexpected from that tall, heavy body, without making a sound, as if she didn't want to attract attention to their presence from everyone else in the house.

Majnun looked at Suzana's arms and back as if he were seeing them for the first time. He had always fixated on other parts of her body. Her arms were round and feminine, and the low-cut back of her blouse revealed the outline of some vertebras of her spine.

Suzana invited him to go directly to her wide, airy bedroom, which looked out over the trees, having him sit in a chair in front of a desk on which rested a few economics books. She sat down on a bed made of dark, reddish wood, crossed her legs, and began to rock one of her feet side to side, while the other, which was on the ground, made nervous noises on the wooden floor. Majnun recalled a verse from the Koran: women should not shake their feet so as not to draw attention to their concealed attractive features.

Suzana took out her ponytail, letting her hair fall naturally about her with a movement of her head. The polish on her fingers and toes was certainly the work of a professional manicurist. With one of her hands fixing her hair, she looked towards the window, displaying her beautiful profile and putting her rosy cheek in high relief.

The desk was ancient, with well-turned curved legs. On the ground, a Persian rug.

What a privilege to be there with her, and alone! She looked the same and looked different, too. Her eyes and lips seemed sweeter than usual.

"Suzana! Oh, Suzana," he said, with more sadness than sensuality.

Suzana looked him in the eyes with a tranquil smile, which provoked in him an emotion composed of fear and hopefulness. He didn't need to unleash his animalistic feelings or try to discover the mysteries of desire. He would take with him the memories of a perfume, a smile, and a topaz-decorated hand that descended down her forehead and covered her eyes, as if she wanted to wipe away some preoccupation. Life seemed like a silent, profound dream.

"Thanks for having me over. I don't want anything more. I'll leave you in peace here and head out."

She reclined further on the bed, supporting herself with her elbows, revealing further her lack of belly fat and the beauty of her smooth, round arms, thrusting her abundant breasts into further relief. It was impossible not to look at the outline of her body, the proportions of an attractive imperfection.

He felt a heaviness in his head and the beating of a tambourine in his heart. Had she perhaps forgiven him? Was she indifferent towards him? Did she think he was ridiculous?

"When I think about all that's happened since we left for Spain, I feel like years have passed. I remember you asked me on the plane what I expected out of the trip. Do you remember? And I told you that I didn't have any expectations, aside from a small break from my normal life. A short break, which I was sure wouldn't have any influence at all on the state of my soul. That nothing in me would change. I truly thought that I would come back the same person. I'd go back to Laila, reunite with my grandpa Dario . . ."

Majnun then made as if to head out the door, his eyes welling with tears. Would he tell Suzana what had happened to him? That he'd nearly been killed?

"I know how much you're suffering," said Suzana, standing up and grabbing his arm.

She leaned her face against his forehead, and he felt his friend's lips lightly graze against a tear that was running down his cheek.

If it weren't for that tear and his suffering, Majnun wouldn't have experienced such joy. We've already said, at another point in the story, that misfortunes can be the origin of joys. Now we can bring this reflection up to date: tears and suffering are also sometimes the very condition of joy.

He tripped over the rugs, shook his head in contempt at his own tactless behavior, and said goodbye, a smile of gratitude on his lips.

Upon arriving back home, his grandma Elvira asked him where he'd been. She had started to look all over for him, assuming the worst.

"Your grandma Mona is also very worried. She already flew back home, but is calling nonstop from São Paulo."

Majnun again burst into tears.

"It's all right, calm down. I know you're very sad. But remember, nothing is set in stone, you're in the bloom of youth, and you have your whole life in front of you."

His whole life in front of him? The same thing that Laila had told him.

He went into his room and shut the door. Why try to shed light into the shadows? Why count the specks of dust in the air? Why try to get someplace? Why desire clarity, control? Why not live in the shadows, accept the road with no definite route, which wasn't even a road at all, just a cleared-out field, open, and opening ever wider?

After two months of recuperation at a clinic, at his grandmother's insistence, he posted on Twitter a thought he'd written down on a scrap of paper and tossed into the shoebox: "The perfect discourse is wordless, the perfect action is inaction. That which is known to all sages is hardly profound."

Rebel with a cause or
how a small movement unleashes great events

A year and a half after his return from Spain, Majnun was taking part in social movements on the internet and preparing for a protest set for June 20th 2013 in Brasilia. He received a call from Carmen via Skype. She was one of the organizers of a protest in front of the Brazilian Embassy in Madrid, which was going to take place on Saturday the 22nd.

Carmen could no longer accuse him of preferring solitude. It's true that he still spent a lot of time in the company of the computer, which — as he put it — didn't shed tears, didn't love, wasn't a demagogue, and didn't order him around. But that wasn't all he did. He felt that he was part of a movement.

"I thought about you these last few days when Snowden revealed that the United States is spying on everyone," he told Carmen on Skype. "All those searches I did on Islamic sites are filed away on American computers, you were totally right."

"Even the conversation we're having now. OK, look, Suzana wrote to me saying that she's making signs for a protest in Brasilia."

"Suzana, huh? I never would have thought."

He hadn't seen Suzana since the day of his grandpa Dario's funeral. How would she react if he called her?

He immediately rang Suzana. Demonstrating enormous enthusiasm for the protest, she accepted Majnun's invitation to stop by his house beforehand. They could make signs together, and she'd give him a ride in her car, which she'd leave a safe distance from the Esplanade of Ministries.

She arrived with three other friends, two guys and a girl. Majnun almost didn't recognize Suzana, perhaps because he hoped to see her in shorts or a miniskirt, not in long pants and a T-shirt, or else because he was unaccustomed to seeing her without makeup. The trunk of the car was full of materials that they set up in his grandpa Dario's old office.

On that day, his grandma Mona and grandpa Sérgio were there visiting and they—as well as his grandma Elvira—felt, as far as Majnun could tell, sympathetic towards the protests, although they didn't understand the purpose of them. While the young people were making final preparations, writing rallying cries on the signs, the grandparents wandered about them, recalling conversations they'd had, there in that very house, when Dario was still alive.

"I feel an enthusiasm in the air similar to that of May of '68 or the 'La movida' movement," said Sérgio.

"Don't exaggerate! These protests don't have anything to do with changing people's behavior," disagreed Elvira. "I see similarities with other recent movements, including those of the Arab Spring and the protest movement in Spain. But only in the surprise of it all, in the possibility that minor incidents can become major ones."

"Not just that," said Majnun. "Also in the will of the people to participate, the jump from social media to the streets, the distrust of political representatives, and in the horizontality of the protests. There are no leaders among us. We're all in the same boat. We're equals."

"It's an advantage that you're all equals and no one is speaking in the name of the people. But you all aren't only protesting about public transportation; the way I see it, the movement goes in a number of directions, and I wouldn't say you are all in the same boat. In time, that discontent is going to need focus and political representation," said Elvira.

"What he's trying to say is that we aren't linked to any sort of organization. We don't belong to a political party. Or unions. We're not beholden to ideologies," said Suzana. "We have concrete demands, things that can be done right now. We want the political system to be more honest and less deceitful. That it follows the rule of law, but not only that, since not everything that is legal is ethical. We have to be exacting. Why not adopt the FIFA pattern of stadiums for public morality? Or for public transportation, health care, education, or public safety?"

"And we're bringing together everyone who wants to protest," added one of the young guys who had come with Suzana.

"Spring is just a beginning and will soon pass by," said Sérgio.

"Like in the Middle East," concluded Elvira.

"But it will return again, you all can be certain of that," refuted Mona.

Sérgio looked at Majnun:

"My question is as follows: if the movement isn't political, man, what meaning does it have?"

"It means another sort of politics," Majnun replied harshly.

He had written out slogans from signs he'd seen on the computer or on TV in São Paulo, Rio, and Recife. From there he extracted what was of greatest interest to him in that spring in autumn. He copied down a few of these slogans, though one of them was featured most prominently: "Sorry for the disturbance. We're changing the country."

"I just hope that these aren't mere disturbances. Or that it doesn't end up like in the novel by Lampedusa: 'It's necessary for things to change, so that everything can stay the same,'" added Sérgio.

On the Esplanada, Majnun, Suzana, and her friends followed the crowd to the Congress building, which was protected by a blockade of policemen. The river of people, furious, were diverted towards Itamaraty Palace. There was a lot of pushing and jostling, Suzana fell down on the grass, and Majnun came over to help her.

"It's nothing serious," she said, but her pants were now stained and her shirt was torn.

When the fire started at Itamaraty Palace, the two of them got separated from their other friends and decided to leave the protest. They started walking down the Eixão highway in the midst of the tumult.

Majnun walked Suzana back to her car. They agreed to get together the next day. She didn't need to pick him up, he would stop by her apartment.

When he arrived the following day, there was music playing, very loudly.

"I'm here alone," she said. "My parents are traveling. So I can turn up the volume on the stereo as loud as I want."

She was nodding her head, as if nodding "yes" over and over, to the sound of a very pronounced beat: "Some kind of nature, some kind of soul, . . . The needy eat mayonnaise, They wear phony clothes . . . Well, me, I like plastics and digital foils . . ." Majnun imitated Suzana's movements, and the two of them performed a dance of the heads.

They danced and danced, Majnun recalling the moment in Madrid when she stopped dancing when he put his hands on her waist. Perhaps her tranquility this time around was due to the fact that she was at home, that she dominated her space.

"I just remembered that once, back in Madrid, we danced together in the hotel."

"Let's just stick to good memories," she said.

"For me it is a good memory."

"Let's not argue about this."

"Are you going to go to Rio for World Youth Day?" Majnun asked.

He had read that seven thousand young people from the Federal District were traveling to Rio for Catholic World Youth Day, set to take place, with Pope Francis in attendance, from July 23rd to the 28th.

"I already felt like an old lady in Madrid, just imagine now! No. I'm going to stick around here. What about Carmen? Any news from her?"

"I talked to her on Skype within the last few days."

"We talk every once in a while, too"

"She's getting by with her catering work."

"At the height of the crisis, she said she sold everything she owned here."

"I even bought her motorcycle. She's thinking about opening a restaurant with a Spanish friend of hers."

"I think that's crazy."

Sitting beside her, he in a polo shirt and new pants and shoes, she in jeans and a red blouse, Majnun looked around the room from one side to the other, admiring the furniture, the paintings, and the rugs. He could hardly believe what was happening. What luck, to be there next to Suzana, monopolizing all of her attention. What joy, to have found such a great, shared affinity for these protests. He, who once thought she was so different from him, had changed his mind. Ultimately, they were kindred spirits. She was putting all her intelligence and preparation, he concluded, into the defense of those causes that would change Brazil.

"I remember you carrying protest signs in Madrid," she said.

"Inconsequential foolishness. This is different."

She opened a bottle of cava.

"And what about Pablo?" asked Majnun.

"I don't see Pablo anymore. He's still in Rio. Back in Madrid we said we were going to take a break, and that break ended up going . . ."

She had various theories about what was happening in Brazil. She talked about police violence, the spark that lit the powder keg. About the economy. About the World Cup and the Olympics, about the lack of investment in public services . . . She didn't even spare her father and his friends in Congress.

She wanted to know what he'd been up to since they'd last seen each other, on the day of his grandpa's funeral.

"I'm finally doing what I want. I'm studying history at the University of Brasilia and teaching history classes at a school."

"Still obsessed with the Moors?"

The conversation went on for hours, to the sound of the music.

How could it be? Was this the same Suzana? Hatred had once separated them. Now affection was bringing them together. Suzana had become more beautiful, he noticed, unlike him, whose appearance had grown gloomier.

"Don't ask me why, but if you promise me you'll behave yourself, I want you to sleep here with me," she said. "You must think I'm a prude, right? But I wouldn't feel good if I had sex with you. I hope you understand."

Strange, the pathways of desire. He'd traveled a long way, from undesired to desired. And what had unleashed this change? A small movement, a gesture, a coincidence, a chance meeting.

Majnun lay down beside Suzana without touching her. He wore only his white linen underwear. Some of her charm was lost in those light blue pajamas, which were baggy and didn't accentuate her body.

"It pleases me to have you here beside me. I just don't want it to turn into anything more than this."

"I like being here beside you, too."

"So are you going to behave yourself?"

"I won't do anything you don't want me to."

She ran her hands over Majnun's hair and then pulled his head over onto her shoulder.

Majnun couldn't control his erection and didn't want to, anyway. So that Suzana wouldn't kick him out of the bed, he avoided pressing his body against hers. Now what was going to happen? He put himself in God's hands — no, not God, who might not like this, but also not into the devil's hands. Maybe there was some open-minded African god who would accept him as he was, with no plans, living in the here and now. What luck, to have a night like that one, even if nothing happened and it was only a single night.

He could hear sounds from the street. People down below the window burst into laughter. A car honked in the parking garage.

"Let's go to sleep," she said without looking at him, then turned off the light on the nightstand.

Majnun gave her a kiss on the shoulder.

When the first light of day started to penetrate the gaps in the blinds, Majnun pulled up the sheet and looked down at Suzana's body stretched out on the bed, still facing away from him. She was deep in sleep. He could smell her perfume. He heard birds warbling outside. Her breathing became heavier, belabored. Was she pretending to be asleep? The birds twittered even louder. She didn't open her eyes, nor say anything, but she sighed.

When she turned towards him, he noticed that her breasts were smaller than when he'd seen them in Madrid; she must have had cosmetic surgery. He turned his body towards her, touching her thighs.

"Oh!" she said

"Didn't mean to."

"That's not what you promised me."

"Sorry."

"You want a lot more than that, don't you?" she asked.

"Like I said, I don't want to do anything you don't want."

Suzana started caressing Majnun's face tenderly.

He took a deep breath.

"I'll give you a massage, but that's it."

She turned on the nightstand light, a feeble light, and went over to look for something in the back of one of dresser drawers. Her pajama bottoms were slightly sagging, allowing the top of her butt to be seen.

She came back with a tube of lotion in her hand.

She sat down on his thighs, leaned over, and kissed him on the lips. She ran her hands up and down over his body, ever faster. The massage was terrible, but the affection was real. He closed his eyes and was unable to contain a gasp.

"You're being good," said Suzana.

Majnun stood up and went to the bathroom. When he came back, Suzana was lying on her back.

"Thanks," he said.

"That's not something you say," she replied.

He turned her towards him, then looked her in the eyes and hugged her. They remained like that for a long time, holding each other close.

He felt relaxed. And his desire had passed.

"Did you like me sleeping here?"

"I did. But it's not going to go any further than that. I want to be your friend."

"Are we going to see each other again?"

"I don't know. If the protests continue . . ." she laughed.

Back home, Majnun took a long shower and then sat down at his grandpa's desk, where he'd brought his laptop. He tried to remember everything important that had happened since he'd decided to travel to Madrid with Carmen and Suzana. He finally understood the meaning of a card he'd pulled out of the deck one day: "Free yourself from desire and hope, for hope is the temporization of the impossible or the putting off of what is already possible."

He took out the papers from his shoebox and his notes for the novella that he continued writing and rewriting. He sent a message to Carmen through Facebook: "I'm back in the world. I've discovered that when we know that everything is coming to an end, we start to understand what is most precious about it. I want you to be my friend forever."

Carmen replied immediately:

"Is everything going all right, my friend? Talk to me."

He thought about saying, like Aragon in his *Crazy about Elsa,* that "every being has as its destiny the misfortune of Granada." He wanted to say that his religion and his faith were love, and repeat along with Aragon the imaginary *surah*: "Oh infidel, you shall not blaspheme the name of the Lord, for He does not exist." And yet "God is in those who negate Him."

A few weeks later, on a Tuesday, after Pope Francis had already left Brazil, having encouraged the revolt and having spoken about marriage, mercy in relation to divorce, a new role for women in the Church, and respect for gays, his grandma introduced him to a young woman, a journalism intern in her early twenties who was researching a piece about his grandpa Dario.

"Maybe you can help her," said Elvira.

"Pleased to meet you. I'm Elsa."

"Elsa?"

Who knew, maybe his passion for Laila could turn into a love that could grow little by little, like a tree that reaches for the sky in many directions. Elsa was there in front of him, wearing a dress that was so clean and well pressed that it seemed like it had just come from the cleaners. It was of a white silk that gave off golden reflections and not very low-cut, though it still revealed the jutting collarbone of a slender body. The thin straps left her shoulders almost naked, her skin a brown color that contrasted with the white of the dress in an attractive manner. "Damn!" he thought. He could erase everything he'd been through and start over. Multiply everything by that magic number, zero. It was moving to see that face looking seriously at him. "Damn!" he thought again.

After they exchanged email addresses and she left, he got out the shoebox, where he added all the scraps of paper accumulated over the course of the trip to the old ones: prolegomena, references, leads, some sparse and incomplete pieces of information which he had stored up the way people hoard trash in the back rooms of a house, sacrificing to perfection neither leftovers, nor absences, nor excesses, nor deformations, neither the ugly nor the dirty. Ideas and pieces of information that could be grouped together in many different ways.

The music of the words—drunken, cruel, basic, savage, virgin— was a constant hum in that uncertain spring. That all this might arise: the inert action, the wordless discourse, words made of silence, as fertile as desperation, capable of translating all of life's mystery, a vertigo of the senses; of summing up fear and anguish, profound ecstasy; of causing a new love to be born. Even if he was only twenty-two years old, his future was immense and he didn't know what pathways existed into the labyrinths of his story.

Indeed, words able to describe pure forms and all the world's inventions, overflowing the borders of texts and acknowledged definitions. Loose, light words that didn't carry thought and yet signified more than the words themselves. Ideas that settled into gentle rhythms, transformed into feathers, weightless and devoid of pride. Words that flashed like a light in his head, delirious, making him dizzy and imperfect. He then recalled *The Book of Sorrows, El libro de Dolores.* He transformed that profound sorrow into more words, latching onto them as if they were a lifeline, then tossing them into his shoebox. All he'd experienced would end up as words. One word, another word, and another still, the novella was made, line after line, like his own life, consisting of a search for meaning, phrases, and of incomplete actions.

JOÃO ALMINO is the author of five novels, of which *The Five Seasons of Love*, *The Book of Emotions*, and *Free City* are available in English translation, the latter two from Dalkey Archive Press. He has taught at UC Berkeley, Stanford, the Autonomous National University of Mexico, and the University of Brasília.

RHETT MCNEIL has translated books by Machado de Assis (*Stories*), António Lobo Antunes (*Splendor of Portugal*), and Gonçalo M. Tavares (*Joseph Walser's Machine*).

MICHAL AJVAZ, *The Golden Age.*
The Other City.

PIERRE ALBERT-BIROT, *Grabinoulor.*

YUZ ALESHKOVSKY, *Kangaroo.*

FELIPE ALFAU, *Chromos.*
Locos.

ANTÓNIO LOBO ANTUNES, *Knowledge of Hell.*
The Splendor of Portugal.

ALAIN ARIAS-MISSON, *Theatre of Incest.*

GABRIELA AVIGUR-ROTEM, *Heatwave and Crazy Birds.*

DJUNA BARNES, *Ladies Almanack.*
Ryder.

DONALD BARTHELME, *The King.*
Paradise.

SVETISLAV BASARA, *Chinese Letter.*

MIQUEL BAUÇÀ, *The Siege in the Room.*

RENÉ BELLETTO, *Dying.*

MAREK BIENCZYK, *Transparency.*

ANDREI BITOV, *Pushkin House.*

ANDREJ BLATNIK, *You Do Understand.*
Law of Desire.

IGNÁCIO DE LOYOLA BRANDÃO,
Anonymous Celebrity.
Zero.

BONNIE BREMSER, *Troia: Mexican Memoirs.*

CHRISTINE BROOKE-ROSE,
Amalgamemnon.

MICHEL BUTOR, *Degrees.*
Mobile.

G. CABRERA INFANTE, *Infante's Inferno.*
Three Trapped Tigers.

JULIETA CAMPOS, *The Fear of Losing Eurydice.*

ANNE CARSON, *Eros the Bittersweet.*

ORLY CASTEL-BLOOM, *Dolly City.*

LOUIS-FERDINAND CÉLINE, *North.*
Conversations with Professor Y.
London Bridge.

MARIE CHAIX, *The Laurels of Lake Constance.*

HUGO CHARTERIS, *The Tide Is Right.*

ERIC CHEVILLARD, *Demolishing Nisard.*
The Author and Me.

MARC CHOLODENKO, *Mordechai Schamz.*

JOSHUA COHEN, *Witz.*

EMILY HOLMES COLEMAN, *The Shutter of Snow.*

ERIC CHEVILLARD, *The Author and Me.*

ROBERT COOVER, *A Night at the Movies.*

STANLEY CRAWFORD, *Log of the S.S. The Mrs Unguentine.*
Some Instructions to My Wife.

RENÉ CREVEL, *Putting My Foot in It.*

RALPH CUSACK, *Cadenza.*

NICHOLAS DELBANCO, *Sherbrookes.*
The Count of Concord.

NIGEL DENNIS, *Cards of Identity.*

PETER DIMOCK, *A Short Rhetoric for Leaving the Family.*

ARIEL DORFMAN, *Konfidenz.*

COLEMAN DOWELL, *Island People.*
Too Much Flesh and Jabez.

ARKADII DRAGOMOSHCHENKO,
Dust.

RIKKI DUCORNET, *Phosphor in Dreamland.*
The Complete Butcher's Tales.
The Fountains of Neptune.

JEAN ECHENOZ, *Chopin's Move.*

FRANÇOIS EMMANUEL, *Invitation to a Voyage.*

PAUL EMOND, *The Dance of a Sham.*

SALVADOR ESPRIU, *Ariadne in the Grotesque Labyrinth.*

JUAN FILLOY, *Op Oloop.*

ANDY FITCH, *Pop Poetics.*

GUSTAVE FLAUBERT, *Bouvard and Pécuchet.*

KASS FLEISHER, *Talking out of School.*

JON FOSSE, *Aliss at the Fire.*
Melancholy.

FORD MADOX FORD, *The March of Literature.*

MAX FRISCH, *I'm Not Stiller.*

Man in the Holocene.

CARLOS FUENTES, *Christopher Unborn.*
  Distant Relations.
  Terra Nostra.
  Where the Air Is Clear.

TAKEHIKO FUKUNAGA, *Flowers of Grass.*

WILLIAM GADDIS, JR., *The Recognitions.*

JANICE GALLOWAY, *Foreign Parts.*
  The Trick Is to Keep Breathing.

WILLIAM H. GASS, *Life Sentences.*
  The Tunnel.
  The World Within the Word.
  Willie Masters' Lonesome Wife.

GÉRARD GAVARRY, *Hoppla! 1 2 3..*

C. S. GISCOMBE, *Giscome Road.*
  Here.

WITOLD GOMBROWICZ, *A Kind of Testament.*

PAULO EMÍLIO SALES GOMES, *P's Three Women.*

GEORGI GOSPODINOV, *Natural Novel.*

JUAN GOYTISOLO, *Count Julian.*
  Juan the Landless.
  Makbara.
  Marks of Identity.

JACK GREEN, *Fire the Bastards!*

JIŘÍ GRUŠA, *The Questionnaire.*

MELA HARTWIG, *Am I a Redundant Human Being?*

JOHN HAWKES, *The Passion Artist.*
  Whistlejacket.

KEIZO HINO, *Isle of Dreams.*

KAZUSHI HOSAKA, *Plainsong.*

NAOYUKI II, *The Shadow of a Blue Cat.*

DRAGO JANČAR, *The Tree with No Name.*

MIKHEIL JAVAKHISHVILI, *Kvachi.*

GERT JONKE, *The Distant Sound.*
  Homage to Czerny.
  The System of Vienna.

JACQUES JOUET, *Mountain R.*
  Savage.
  Upstaged.

MIEKO KANAI, *The Word Book.*

YORAM KANIUK, *Life on Sandpaper.*

ZURAB KARUMIDZE, *Dagny.*

JOHN KELLY, *From Out of the City.*

HUGH KENNER, *Flaubert, Joyce and Beckett: The Stoic Comedians.*
  Joyce's Voices.

DANILO KIŠ, *The Attic.*
  The Lute and the Scars.
  Psalm 44.
  A Tomb for Boris Davidovich.

ANITA KONKKA, *A Fool's Paradise.*

GEORGE KONRÁD, *The City Builder.*

TADEUSZ KONWICKI, *A Minor Apocalypse.*
  The Polish Complex.

ANNA KORDZAIA-SAMADASHVILI, *Me, Margarita.*

MENIS KOUMANDAREAS, *Koula.*

ELAINE KRAF, *The Princess of 72nd Street.*

JIM KRUSOE, *Iceland.*

AYSE KULIN, *Farewell: A Mansion in Occupied Istanbul.*

EMILIO LASCANO TEGUI, *On Elegance While Sleeping.*

ERIC LAURRENT, *Do Not Touch.*

VIOLETTE LEDUC, *La Bâtarde.*

EDOUARD LEVÉ, *Autoportrait.*
  Newspaper.
  Suicide.
  Works.

MARIO LEVI, *Istanbul Was a Fairy Tale.*

DEBORAH LEVY, *Billy and Girl.*

JOSÉ LEZAMA LIMA, *Paradiso.*

ROSA LIKSOM, *Dark Paradise.*

OSMAN LINS, *Avalovara.*
  The Queen of the Prisons of Greece.

FLORIAN LIPUŠ, *The Errors of Young Tjaž.*

GORDON LISH, *Peru.*

ALF MACLOCHLAINN, *Out of Focus.*
  Past Habitual.
  The Corpus in the Library.

RON LOEWINSOHN, *Magnetic Field(s).*

YURI LOTMAN, *Non-Memoirs.*

MINA LOY, *Stories and Essays of Mina Loy.*
MICHELINE AHARONIAN MARCOM,
 A Brief History of Yes.
 The Mirror in the Well.
BEN MARCUS, *The Age of Wire and String.*
DAVID MARKSON, *Reader's Block.*
 Wittgenstein's Mistress.
CAROLE MASO, *AVA.*
HARRY MATHEWS, *Cigarettes.*
 The Conversions.
 The Journalist.
 My Life in CIA.
 Singular Pleasures.
 Tlooth.
HISAKI MATSUURA, *Triangle.*
ABDELWAHAB MEDDEB, *Talismano.*
GERHARD MEIER, *Isle of the Dead.*
HERMAN MELVILLE, *The Confidence-Man.*
AMANDA MICHALOPOULOU, *I'd Like.*
CHRISTINE MONTALBETTI, *The Origin of Man.*
 Western.
WARREN MOTTE, *Fables of the Novel: French Fiction since 1990.*
 Fiction Now: The French Novel in the 21st Century.
 Mirror Gazing.
 Oulipo: A Primer of Potential Literature.
GERALD MURNANE, *Barley Patch.*
 Inland.
YVES NAVARRE, *Our Share of Time.*
 Sweet Tooth.
DOROTHY NELSON, *In Night's City.*
 Tar and Feathers.
WILFRIDO D. NOLLEDO, *But for the Lovers.*
FLANN O'BRIEN, *At Swim-Two-Birds.*
 The Best of Myles.
 The Dalkey Archive.
 The Hard Life.
 The Poor Mouth.
 The Third Policeman.
CLAUDE OLLIER, *The Mise-en-Scène.*
 Wert and the Life Without End.
PATRIK OUŘEDNÍK, *Europeana.*

The Opportune Moment, 1855.
BORIS PAHOR, *Necropolis.*
FERNANDO DEL PASO, *News from the Empire.*
 Palinuro of Mexico.
ROBERT PINGET, *The Inquisitory.*
 Mahu or The Material.
 Trio.
MANUEL PUIG, *Betrayed by Rita Hayworth.*
 The Buenos Aires Affair.
 Heartbreak Tango.
RAYMOND QUENEAU, *The Last Days.*
 Odile.
 Pierrot Mon Ami.
 Saint Glinglin.
ANN QUIN, *Berg.*
 Passages.
 Three.
 Tripticks.
ISHMAEL REED, *The Free-Lance Pallbearers.*
 The Last Days of Louisiana Red.
 Ishmael Reed: The Plays.
 Juice!
 The Terrible Threes.
 The Terrible Twos.
 Yellow Back Radio Broke-Down.
JASIA REICHARDT, *15 Journeys Warsaw to London.*
JOÃO UBALDO RIBEIRO, *House of the Fortunate Buddhas.*
RAINER MARIA RILKE,
 The Notebooks of Malte Laurids Brigge.
JULIÁN RÍOS, *The House of Ulysses.*
 Larva: A Midsummer Night's Babel.
 Poundemonium.
ALAIN ROBBE-GRILLET, *Project for a Revolution in New York.*
 A Sentimental Novel.
AUGUSTO ROA BASTOS, *I the Supreme.*
DANIËL ROBBERECHTS, *Arriving in Avignon.*
JEAN ROLIN, *The Explosion of the Radiator Hose.*
OLIVIER ROLIN, *Hotel Crystal.*

ALIX CLEO ROUBAUD, *Alix's Journal.*

RAYMOND ROUSSEL, *Impressions of Africa.*

VEDRANA RUDAN, *Night.*

PABLO M. RUIZ, *Four Cold Chapters on the Possibility of Literature.*

GERMAN SADULAEV, *The Maya Pill.*

LUIS RAFAEL SÁNCHEZ, *Macho Camacho's Beat.*

SEVERO SARDUY, *Cobra & Maitreya.*

NATHALIE SARRAUTE, *Do You Hear Them?*
Martereau.
The Planetarium.

STIG SÆTERBAKKEN, *Siamese.*
Self-Control.
Through the Night.

VIKTOR SHKLOVSKY, *Bowstring.*
Literature and Cinematography.
Theory of Prose.
Third Factory.

PIERRE SINIAC, *The Collaborators.*

KJERSTI A. SKOMSVOLD, *The Faster I Walk, the Smaller I Am.*

JOSEF ŠKVORECKÝ, *The Engineer of Human Souls.*

GILBERT SORRENTINO, *Aberration of Starlight.*
Blue Pastoral.
Steelwork.
Under the Shadow.

MARKO SOSIČ, *Ballerina, Ballerina.*

ANDRZEJ STASIUK, *Dukla.*
Fado.

GERTRUDE STEIN, *The Making of Americans.*
A Novel of Thank You.

LARS SVENDSEN, *A Philosophy of Evil.*

PIOTR SZEWC, *Annihilation.*

GONÇALO M. TAVARES, *A Man: Klaus Klump.*
Jerusalem.
Learning to Pray in the Age of Technique.

LUCIAN DAN TEODOROVICI, *Our Circus Presents . . .*

NIKANOR TERATOLOGEN, *Assisted Living.*

DUMITRU TSEPENEAG, *Hotel Europa.*
The Necessary Marriage.
Pigeon Post.
Vain Art of the Fugue.

ESTHER TUSQUETS, *Stranded.*

DUBRAVKA UGRESIC, *Lend Me Your Character.*
Thank You for Not Reading.

TOR ULVEN, *Replacement.*

MATI UNT, *Brecht at Night.*
Diary of a Blood Donor.
Things in the Night.

ÁLVARO URIBE & OLIVIA SEARS, EDS., *Best of Contemporary Mexican Fiction.*

ELOY URROZ, *Friction.*
The Obstacles.

LUISA VALENZUELA, *Dark Desires and the Others.*
He Who Searches.

BORIS VIAN, *Heartsnatcher.*

LLORENÇ VILLALONGA, *The Dolls' Room.*

TOOMAS VINT, *An Unending Landscape.*

AUSTRYN WAINHOUSE, *Hedyphagetica.*

DIANE WILLIAMS,
Excitability: Selected Stories.
Romancer Erector.

MARGUERITE YOUNG, *Angel in the Forest.*
Miss MacIntosh, My Darling.

REYOUNG, *Unbabbling.*

VLADO ŽABOT, *The Succubus.*

ZORAN ŽIVKOVIĆ , *Hidden Camera.*

LOUIS ZUKOFSKY, *Collected Fiction.*

VITOMIL ZUPAN, *Minuet for Guitar.*

SCOTT ZWIREN, *God Head.*

AND MORE . . .